Summer's laughter was refreshing and...beautiful

But then, Mack realized, *she* was beautiful. Her eyes were big and beguiling. Her hair shone like golden wheat at sunset. Mack groaned inwardly, thinking he'd gone all soft and poetic, just watching the woman. But he couldn't stop watching her.

Until a big goose flapped his wings and started seriously chasing Summer. Suddenly she was surrounded by quacking, hungry geese, ducks and ducklings.

"Hey, do something. I'm being attacked," Summer said to him as she rushed by.

Mack shook his head, his own laughter relieving some of the tension. "I'm enjoying this too much."

He grabbed her hand and urged her toward the building. They stopped at the veranda, laughing as they tried to catch their breaths.

Summer gazed at Mack, her eyes shining with mirth. "I've never been rescued from ducks and geese before."

Mack realized he'd made a fatal mistake. He shouldn't have taken her by the hand, because now he didn't want to let go. Ever.

Books by Lenora Worth

Love Inspired

Steeple Hill Books

LENORA WORTH

grew up in a small Georgia town and decided in the fourth grade that she wanted to be a writer. But first she married her high school sweetheart, then moved to Atlanta, Georgia. Taking care of their baby daughter at home while her husband worked at night, Lenora discovered the world of romance novels and knew that's what she wanted to write. And so she began.

In 1993, Lenora's hard work and determination finally paid off with that first sale. "I never gave up, and I believe my faith in God helped get me through the rough times when I doubted myself," Lenora says. "Each time I start a new book, I say a prayer, asking God to give me the strength and direction to put the words to paper. That's why I'm so thrilled to be a part of Steeple Hill's Love Inspired line, where I can combine my faith in God with my love of romance. It's the best combination."

A PERFECT LOVE

LENORA WORTH

Steeple
Hill®

Published by Steeple Hill Books™

If you purchased this book without a cover you should be aware that this book is stolen property. It was reported as "unsold and destroyed" to the publisher, and neither the author nor the publisher has received any payment for this "stripped book."

STEEPLE HILL BOOKS

Steeple
Hill®

ISBN 0-373-81244-2

A PERFECT LOVE

Copyright © 2005 by Lenora H. Nazworth

All rights reserved. Except for use in any review, the reproduction or utilization of this work in whole or in part in any form by any electronic, mechanical or other means, now known or hereafter invented, including xerography, photocopying and recording, or in any information storage or retrieval system, is forbidden without the written permission of the editorial office, Steeple Hill Books, 233 Broadway, New York, NY 10279 U.S.A.

All characters in this book have no existence outside the imagination of the author and have no relation whatsoever to anyone bearing the same name or names. They are not even distantly inspired by any individual known or unknown to the author, and all incidents are pure invention.

This edition published by arrangement with Steeple Hill Books.

® and TM are trademarks of Steeple Hill Books, used under license. Trademarks indicated with ® are registered in the United States Patent and Trademark Office, the Canadian Trade Marks Office and in other countries.

www.SteepleHill.com

Printed in U.S.A.

There is no fear in love,
but perfect love casts out fear.
—*1 John* 4:18

To my niece, Jessica Smith, with lots of love.

Chapter One

This wasn't the best place in the world to have a breakdown, either in one's car or one's life.

Summer Maxwell was having both, however.

Wanting to say words her grandmother wouldn't appreciate, Summer kicked the front right tire of her late-model sportscar, then let out a frustrated groan as she looked up and down the lonely Texas back road. A sign a few feet from her car stated Athens, 9 Miles.

So close, yet still so far away.

"I just had to *drive* all the way home from New York, didn't I?" she shouted to the hot, humid wind. "And I just had to do it in this pitiful excuse for an automobile."

Summer eyed the faded red of the twenty-year-old Jaguar, wondering why she'd never bothered to buy a new car. Maybe because this one had belonged to her father at one time, and maybe because that was a connection she wasn't ready to give up, even if it wasn't always pleasant.

James Maxwell had given his only daughter the car when she'd graduated from high school, his silky, charming words making the deal all the more sweet since he'd missed the graduation ceremony. "Daddy wants you to have this one, honey. I'm getting me a brand-new Porsche. And your mama, she doesn't want this one. Guess that means I'll be buying her a Cadillac soon."

"Yeah, you sure did buy Mama a new set of wheels," Summer muttered as the gloaming of another hot Texas day brought a cool wisp of breeze floating over her. And James Maxwell hadn't even bothered to wish his daughter well as she headed off to college with her cousins, April and Autumn. No, her father hadn't bothered with much at all regarding his daughter. Maybe because he'd wanted a son so badly, to carry on the glory days of his rodeo career.

"Sorry, Daddy," Summer said now and wondered why she always felt it necessary to apologize for everything.

Her parents were globe-trotters, too tied up in each other and her father's rodeo and oil-industry endorsements to worry about their rebellious daughter. So they'd dumped her on her mother's parents for most of her life, while they enjoyed the good life that came with being oil- and cattle-rich Maxwells.

"I'm almost there, Memaw," Summer said as she lifted the hot hood of the car, then backed away as a damp mist of smoke poured over her. "Must be the radiator again."

Wishing she hadn't been so stubborn about *not* flying, or about *not* taking her cousin Autumn's sensible sedan, Summer looked up and down the long road. She could call her grandfather on her cell, get him to come and pick her up. That is, if her cell would even work in these isolated piney woods.

"Or I could walk," she reasoned. "Maybe physical activity would keep me from having that breakdown I so richly deserve."

Grabbing her aged baseball-glove-leather tote bag from the passenger's seat of the convertible, Summer tried her cell. Low power and even lower battery. No surprise there.

"Okay, I guess I get to walk nine miles along this bug-infested highway. Nice, Summer, real nice."

She was about to put up the worn black top of the car and lock it, when she heard a truck rumbling along the highway.

"Oh, great. Let's hope you are a kind soul," she said into the wind. "'I have always relied upon the kindness of strangers'", she quoted from Tennessee Williams.

And let's pray you aren't some psycho out on the loose. Not that she couldn't handle herself. She was armed with pepper spray and a whole arsenal of self-defense courses. She'd learned all about how to protect herself, working as a counselor to battered women at a New York City YWCA for the past five years.

She'd also learned all about the dark, evil side of life working there, too. Which was why she was now stranded on this road. Everyone she knew in New York, including her cousins and her immediate supervisor, had agreed it was time for Summer to take a vacation.

Burned out. Stressed out. Angry. Bitter.

Those were the words they'd used to describe her.

And that didn't even begin to touch the surface.

Summer took a long breath, tried to imagine a peaceful scene somewhere in the tired recesses of her mind, while she waited for the old truck to pull up beside her. But somehow, she didn't believe deep breathing would get her through this acute, aching depression.

And neither would God, she decided.

Then she looked up and saw her rescuer.

He was young, probably only a few years older than Summer's twenty-seven years. He was pretty in a rugged, rough-cut way. He had vivid gray-blue eyes that flashed like heat lightning. And he had crisp, curly light-brown hair that seemed to be rebelling against the humidity.

Warning flares went off in Summer's weary mind like fireworks on the Fourth of July.

Putting the rickety old truck into Park, he said, "Need some help?"

Summer decided that was an under-statement, but she hid that behind what she hoped was a serene smile. "Kinda looks that way, doesn't it?"

"Want me to look under the hood?"

"No need," she said, ignoring the home-sick delight his Texas drawl caused along her skin. "It's the radiator. Probably finally busted for good."

He got out and walked to the raised hood anyway. Since he was a man, Summer figured he didn't trust her word on car maintenance. Had to see it for himself. Probably thought just because she was a blonde, that she didn't have any brain cells. Never mind that she had been a double major in college. No need for this handsome interloper to know that just yet.

He turned and wiped his hands down the sides of his worn jeans. "Yep, looks like you're right. It's too hot to even touch right now."

Summer noted his solid build and laid-back swagger. "I told you so," she said with a hint of sarcasm to hide the hint of interest she had in him.

He ignored the sarcasm, his gaze filled with his own interest. "Where you headed?"

"Athens." She didn't feel the need to give him any more information.

"I live there," he said. Then he extended his hand. "Mack Riley."

"Summer Maxwell," she said, taking his hand and enjoying the strength of his touch a little too much.

He pulled his hand away with a quick tug, making her wonder if he'd felt that little bit of awareness, too. "Summer?"

"Yes," she said, thinking she saw recognition in his beautiful eyes.

"Pretty name." He hesitated, then said, "And just who are you visiting in Athens?"

"My grandparents," she replied, mystified by his suddenly odd behavior. "I wanted to surprise them."

"Oh, I reckon they'll be surprised, all right," he said as he shut the car's hood. "Who are your grandparents? I might know them."

"Jesse and Martha Creswell," Summer said, thinking he probably did know them. Everybody knew just about everybody else in the small town of Athens, Texas.

He stepped back, gave her a look that shouted confusion and surprise. "Well, how 'bout that."

"You know them?" she asked, echoing her thoughts.

"I sure do," he replied. "Good people. C'mon, I'll give you a ride into town, then we'll send a tow truck to get your car."

"I'd appreciate that," Summer said, sending up a prayer that he wasn't dangerous. She knew better then to get in a car with a complete stranger, but he seemed normal, and he knew her grandparents. But just to test that theory, she put her hands on her hips and asked, "Will I be safe with you?"

He laughed, shook his head. "I'm not on any Top Ten Most Wanted List, if that's what you mean."

Oh, but he could be on a Top Ten Hunk list, Summer decided. His smile was criminal in its beauty.

"Okay," she retorted as she started locking up the car. "I just had to be sure. 'Cause my granddaddy, he shoots first and asks questions later."

"I hear that," he said, helping her to latch the convertible top. "I do believe Jesse would have my hide if I let anything happen to you."

"So how well *do* you know my grandparents?"

"I met them when I first moved here."

Why did she get the feeling he was being evasive? Maybe because he wouldn't look her in the eyes. And maybe because she'd learned not to trust people on first impressions.

"Am I missing something here?" she

asked, determination causing her to dig in her heels.

"Do you have suitcases?" he asked back, misunderstanding the question, maybe on purpose.

"Oh, yes, I do." She unlocked the trunk.

He laughed as he looked down at the beat-up brown leather duffel bag. "How'd you ever get that in this poor excuse for a trunk?"

"You'd be surprised just how much this trunk can hold."

He nodded, grabbed the considerably heavy bag without even a huff of breath, then tossed it in the back of his truck. "Well, I guess that's it then."

"I guess so," she said as she rounded the truck to get in. Once he was all settled behind the wheel, Summer stood at her open door, glaring at him. "Except the part you're leaving out."

He lifted his brow. "Excuse me?"

"You're not telling me the whole story here, are you, Mr. Riley? And I'm not going anywhere with you until you do."

"Call me Mack," he replied, a look of re-solve coloring his eyes. He cranked the truck, motioned toward the seat. "And I don't understand what you're talking about."

Summer had learned all about deceit on the streets of New York, from working with women who lived through the worst kind of deception and deprivation. She could smell it a mile away. "I think you know more about my grandparents than you're telling me. And I want to hear the truth, all of it."

He let out a long sigh, as if he didn't know how to handle such a direct state-ment. "I said I know them. Can't that be enough for now?"

"Nope," Summer replied, smiling sweetly. "You might not be dangerous or a wanted man, but you're being mighty quiet about my grandparents. And I want to know why."

He looked up and down the long road, then nodded. "I guess you deserve an ex-planation. Get in and I'll give you one, I promise."

* * *

Mack Riley stared over at the assertive, no-nonsense woman sitting in his truck. She was a looker, no doubt about that. He'd heard enough about Summer Maxwell to know, though, that all that long blond hair and those bright-blue eyes couldn't hide the fact that she was also very intelligent and sharp.

Too sharp. And right now, not too trusting, either.

What was he supposed to tell the woman? That he knew her grandparents on a first-name basis. That he also knew her rich, jet-setting parents, through conversations with Jesse and Martha, and through having met them on the rare occasions they decided to drop in and check on Summer's grandparents. That he recognized her now, from the many pictures of her growing up that Martha had displayed in her living room. And that he knew enough about Summer herself to fill a book and his own needy imagination.

Mack wasn't ready to open up and have a heart-to-heart with this intriguing woman.

Not yet. So he did what he'd always been so very good at doing. He tried to avoid the issue.

"I'm waiting," Summer said, causing him to glance over at her.

He tried to deflect that in-your-face-look. "Honestly, I don't know what to say, or where to begin. Okay, I do know your folks—real well. Is that a crime?"

"Oh, no," she said, folding her arms as she stared at him. "The crime would be in you withholding information from me. And I think you are. You said you'd explain things. So start talking. Just tell me—is one of them sick? Has something happened, something terrible, that I don't know about?"

Mack made a turn onto yet another long highway. "They're both just fine," he said. "But…a lot has happened over the last few months. When was the last time you talked to them?"

"I saw them at Uncle Stuart's funeral," Summer replied, her blue eyes going dark. "They invited me to come home for a visit.

I told them I'd think about it. I did, and so here I am."

"That funeral was over two months ago," he said, reasoning that she might not know all that had happened since then after all.

"Yes. But they both seemed fine, in good health. Of course, we were all upset about Uncle Stuart."

"So you didn't call ahead, to let them know you were coming?"

She squirmed a bit. "No. I didn't want them to worry since I decided to drive across the country. I wanted to take my time, do a little sightseeing."

Mack got the feeling she hadn't noticed the scenery on her long trip home. Maybe she'd just needed some down time.

He could understand that.

"Well, they'll be surprised, that's for sure."

Then he witnessed some of that famous temper Martha had told him about.

"Listen, mister, I'm getting very bad vibes here. You're scaring me. If there's something I need to know about my grandparents, good or bad, then you'd better spit it out."

Mack stopped the truck in front of the old two-story white farmhouse that had been the Creswell home for many years.

Summer looked up at the house. "Oh, we're here."

"Yes," he said, hating to be the one to break the news to her. "But…there is something you need to know."

"I knew it," she said, her expression grim. "Something bad *has* happened, right?"

Mack looked at the house, then back to Summer Maxwell, deciding he'd have to be up front with her. There was just no other way. "Depends on how you look at things," he said, his fingers tapping on the steering wheel.

"Because?"

"Because, well, Summer, your grandparents no longer own this house."

"What?" She opened the door of the truck and ran around to stand in the tree-lined yard, her gaze moving from him to the house and back. "What do you mean?"

she asked as she turned and stomped back to him.

Mack got out of the truck, dread filling his heart. "I mean, your grandparents decided to sell out and move. Your dad bought them this fancy patio apartment in a new retirement village about a mile up the road."

"He did what?" Summer shouted, her vivid eyes flashing a fire that only added to her obviously fiery nature. "I can't believe this! He sold their *home?* How could he do that? Memaw and Papaw have lived here for over fifty years."

"I know," Mack said, wishing he could soften this news for her. "I know all about this house."

"Oh, yeah. And how come you know so much about all of this?"

Mack glanced at the house, then down at his scuffed work boots. Then he lifted his head and looked straight into Summer's fighting-mad blue eyes.

"Because I own it now," he said. "Your daddy sold this house and the surrounding land to me."

Chapter Two

Summer blinked. "I'm sorry. I don't think I heard you right? Did you say *you* own this house now?"

Mack Riley nodded, shifted his feet, let out a long sigh. "I bought it fair and square about a month ago."

Summer blew at the wispy bangs slanting across her face, one hand on her hip as she wondered whether just to let him have it and get it over with, or wait and attack her father instead. "Fair and square? *Fair and square?* Yeah, I'll just bet my father sold it to you fair and square. How in the world did he get them to agree to this?"

Mack stepped closer, holding his hands

out palms up, as if to protect himself. Which wasn't a bad idea right now, by Summer's way of thinking. "Your grandparents seem happy with the arrangement. In case you haven't noticed, this house is old and in great need of repair, and…well, your grandparents are in about the same shape."

She advanced. "And just who are you to be telling me about my own grandparents?"

He stepped closer, no fear in his eyes. More like defiance and that resolve she'd seen earlier. Which only made Summer even more mad.

"I'll tell you who I am," he said. "I'm about the only one around here who does know about your grandparents. You see, I talk to them on pretty much a daily basis. Your father and mother call every now and then, and you…well, you said yourself you haven't seen them or talked with them since your uncle's funeral. So that leaves me. And believe me, I think they are better off in that retirement village. At least there, they're among friends and near qualified people who can help them."

Summer couldn't believe he was standing here preaching to her! "Oh, well, excuse me. Since you obviously know so very much about my shortcomings, and since you are such a saint for watching over my grandparents, I guess that gives you every right to just bully them out of their home."

"I didn't bully anybody," he retorted, his voice low and full of frustration. "I liked the house and knew it was where I wanted to live. So I bought it."

"Fair and square, of course."

"Yes. I made them a good offer and they took it. It's that simple."

Summer stomped to the truck to get her duffel bag. "Oh, there is nothing simple about this. This…this isn't right. But then, I should have known a man in cahoots with my wayward father wouldn't understand the implications of something so horrible."

"Hey, hold on," Mack said, taking the bag right out of her hand with surprising ease. "I'm not in cahoots with anyone. I just moved here and needed a place to live.

So I bought this house from your father. End of story."

Summer tapped her platform sneaker against the aged wooden steps of the house, her blood boiling just like the radiator on her car had been doing earlier. She could almost feel the hot steam coming out of her ears. "Oh, I think there is much more to this story, and I intend to find out the whole truth."

Such as, how had her father become the spokesperson for her grandparents, and if the house was in such bad repair, why hadn't James Maxwell forked over the funds to renovate his in-laws' home? It just didn't make any sense. But lately, nothing much in her life had made any sense.

She turned and headed to the house, then stopped, hitting a palm to her forehead. "Silly me. I can't stay here *now*. Not with you." Then she plopped down on the steps and looked up at him. "I don't have anywhere to go."

Mack had never seen a more dejected sight. A beautiful, uptown blonde in worn jeans and strange shoes, sitting on the broken steps of a hundred-year-old farmhouse, her eyes brilliant with tears she refused to shed, her expression bordering on outrage, and…her hands trembling slightly as she dropped them over her knees.

All of his protective instincts surfaced, reminding him that he'd come here to find some peace and quiet, not get tangled up in a family squabble. But he had to help her, even if she was fighting mad at him, and the world in general. If for no other reason than to get her off his doorstep.

Thinking she didn't look so bad sitting there, however, he said, "Look, you know there's plenty of room in the house."

"I can't stay here with you," she repeated, gritting the words between her clenched teeth. "First, I'd rather eat nails than do that, and second, this is a small, old-fashioned town. I wouldn't want my grandparents to hear any rumors."

"I admire your stand," Mack said, daring to sit down on the bottom step. "But even if you did want to stay here, the house is being renovated. There's very little furniture and the plumbing is barely working. I'm not even living here full-time myself right now. How about you get a room at that motel out on the highway?"

"How about that?" she said, hitting her hand on her knee. "Great, just great. I look forward to a visit home and I get to stay in some fleabag motel. That should help my burnout and stress level a lot."

Mack could recognize all the signs of her type-A personality. She was a live one. And she looked just about ready to explode into a doozy of a meltdown. The dark circles under her pretty eyes only reminded him of a time when he'd felt the same way. But he sure didn't know how to help her. Or maybe he was just afraid to help her.

Then Mack lifted his head and glanced over at her. "Hey, what about your parents' house? They're in Mexico, last I heard. Won't be home all summer."

Summer groaned, laid her head in her hands. "Go to my parents' house? Oh, that's just peachy. I hate that overblown facade of a house. All that modern art and fake-rustic country-French charm? Like I want to stay at that overpriced country club of a house!"

"It's a nice house," Mack said, thinking it had probably set her parents back a cool million, at least. "And it's safe—"

"Oh, I know all about the gated community and the exclusive homeowner's policy, and the golf course and the country club. My mother fairly gushed about it… last time I bothered to talk to her."

"What is it with you and not talking to your relatives?"

She laughed, the sound bubbling up in her throat like a fresh waterfall hitting rock. "I guess my grandparents didn't let you in on all the family history, after all. We're a bit…estranged, my parents and me."

"Oh, yeah? And why is that?"

Summer pushed at the thick blond hair cascading around her face and shoulders. "Oh, I don't know. Maybe because they never had any time for me when I was growing up, so now I make it a point never to make any time for them." Then she gave him a hard glare. "And besides, that's none of your business."

He knew he was heading into deep water, but he didn't get it. "Your parents seem like nice folks. The times I've been around them—which is few, I'll admit—they seem to be happy and fun-loving. I wish I had their kind of carefree energy."

She gave him a harsh frown. "And I wish they'd use some of that fun-loving, happy, carefree energy on staying in one place. Just once, I wish they'd settle down and actually notice that they have a daughter."

"You have issues, don't you?"

"More than you can imagine, buddy."

"So what are you gonna do?"

She kept staring at him long enough to allow Mack plenty of time to get caught up in the blue of her eyes. "I want to see my grandparents, make sure this is really what they wanted."

"It is, I promise."

She jumped up, pointed a finger in his face. "I don't believe in promises, understand? I've been promised so many things that didn't work out, it's sickening."

"Well, I keep my promises, and I'm telling you, Jesse and Martha are doing better than ever."

"I need to see them," she said again, her voice going all soft and husky. "I can't explain things with my parents—it's a long story and it's something I have to come to terms with. But…I can tell you that I love my grandparents, and I came home to see them. So can I please just do that, go and see them?"

That gentle plea melted Mack's defenses with all the slow-moving force of butter meeting honey on a biscuit, and he knew he was a goner. "Want me to take you to Golden Vista?" At her puzzled, raised-eyebrow expression, he added, "The retirement community where your grandparents live."

"Golden Vista? That just sounds depressing."

"It's a nice place. I think your father invested heavily in—"

Summer shot around him, her long-nailed fingers flailing out into the air. "Oh, I get it now. My father invested in this fancy retirement home, so he's just making sure he covers his assets, right? By forcing my mother's parents to go and *live* there? He just gets lower than a snake's belly with every passing day."

Mack didn't know how to deal with so much bitterness and anger spewing from such a sweet-looking mouth. Although there was a time when he'd been the same way, he reminded himself. But not anymore. "I don't think—"

"I'm not asking you to think," she countered. "Just give me a ride to this…Grim Reaper Vista."

"It's Golden Vista," he said, hiding a grin behind a cough. At least she was entertaining—in a Texas twister kind of way.

"Whatever. Just get me to my grandparents. I'll handle things from there."

Mack could only imagine how this bundle of blond dynamite would handle things.

Not very well, from the looks of her. There was sure to be a whole lot of fallout and carnage left along her pretty, pithy path.

Just one more thing for him to worry about.

One more thing he really didn't need to be worrying about right now.

"So this is Golden Vista?"

At Mack's nod, Summer looked around at the rows and rows of compact wood and brick apartments set against the gentle, rolling hills of East Texas. "It looks like some cookie-cutter type of torture chamber or prison."

Mack grinned over at her, which only made her fold her arms across her waist in defiance. She didn't want to like him. In fact, she refused to like him. He was the enemy.

"It's not a torture chamber and it's certainly not a prison," he said as he guided the truck up a tree-shaded drive. "The residents here aren't in a nursing home. It's called a retirement village. It's a community, completely self-contained. And very secure. It has lots of benefits for people like your grandparents, looking for a place to retire."

"I'll just bet. Retired, as in, shuffleboard in the morning and bingo in the afternoon. My grandparents are probably bored to tears!"

"I'm telling you, they love it," Mack replied. "They can come and go as they please, and Jesse and Martha do just that. They have a new car—"

"Courtesy of my generous father, I reckon?"

"Uh, yes. It's a sturdy sedan."

"And I guess they just love it, too, right?"

"They seem to. I see them gallivanting all over town in it."

"My grandparents do not gallivant."

"Oh, yes, they do."

"Oh, that's right. I forgot you know more about their lifestyle than I do, because I haven't bothered to keep up with them."

"That about tells it like it is," he said, but he held up a hand at her warning glare. "Look, as you so sweetly pointed out, it's none of my business, your relationship with your folks. I can only tell you what

I've seen in the last few weeks since I moved here. They were lonely and they're getting on in years. That farmhouse is kind of isolated out there on the edge of town. I've visited them several times since I moved into the house, just to let them see how the renovations are coming along, and they seem very content at Golden Vista."

"I can't picture that," Summer said, remembering how her grandfather loved to plant a big garden, just so he could give his crop away to half of Henderson County. And her grandmother—she loved to cook and quilt, can vegetables and sew pillows, make clothes and crafts. How could she do all those things cooped up in some cracker box of an apartment?

Summer dropped her head into her hand. "I just have to talk to them."

Mack stopped the truck, then pointed toward a huge, park-like courtyard in the middle of the complex. "Well, there they are, right over there."

Summer looked up to find a large group of senior citizens milling around in Hawaiian shirts and straw hats. Tiki torches burned all around the festive courtyard, while island music played from a loud-speaker. The smell of grilled meat hit the air, reminding her she hadn't eaten since breakfast.

"What in the world?"

"It's a luau," Mack said. "They have these theme parties once a month. Last month, it was Texas barbecue, and I think next month is Summer Gospel Jam—"

"I've heard enough," Summer said, opening the rickety truck door with a knuckle-crunching yank. "I'm going to get to the bottom of this mess."

"Yes, ma'am," Mack said, his grin widening.

"Do you find this humorous?" Summer asked as they met in front of the truck.

"Kinda," he said, then he turned more serious.

Probably because she had murder in her eyes. "I'd advise you to stop grinning."

He did. "You don't like change, do you?"

She lifted a brow. "I can handle change just fine, thank you. What I don't like is when people manipulate my perfectly respectable, God-fearing grandparents. Especially when it's my own parents."

"I don't think they were manipulated," Mack said as he pulled her toward the feisty-looking group of old people. "I think they just got tired of the upkeep on the house and farm, and they decided to relax and have some fun."

"It's just horrible," Summer retorted, not buying his explanation at all. "You're laughing about a situation I find very serious."

"Well, maybe you just take things way *too* seriously."

She stopped, blocking his way toward the party. "My poor, hardworking grandparents are trapped in this…this one-foot-in-the-grave travel stop. And I refuse to believe—"

"Summer? Is that my sweet baby, Summer?"

Summer stopped in midsentence, then turned to stare at the stout woman running…well, gently jogging…toward her. "Memaw?"

"It's me, suga'. Land's sake, we didn't know you were coming for a visit. C'mere and give your old granny a good hug."

Summer took in the hot-pink flamingoes posed across the wide berth of her grandmother's floral muumuu, took in the bright yellow of the shiny plastic lei draping her memaw's neck, then glanced down at her grandmother's feet.

"Memaw, are you wearing kitten-heeled flip-flops?"

"Ain't they cute?" Martha Creswell said as she enveloped Summer in a hug that only a grandmother could get away with. "And take a look at my pedicure," she said as she wrapped her arms around Summer. "My toenails are sparkling—Glistening Party Pink, I think the beautician called it."

Her grandmother's tight-gripped hug just about smothered Summer, but the sweet, familiar scent of Jergens lotion caused tears to brim in Summer's eyes. She pulled away to smile down at her petite grandmother. "Oh, Memaw, what have they done to you?"

"Not a thing," Martha replied, laughing out loud. "Honey, I'm fine, just fine. But wait until you see your grandpa, sugar. He's been on that new diet, don't you know. Trim and slim and wired for action."

"Wired for action? Papaw?" Summer had a bad feeling about this whole setup. A very bad feeling.

Chapter Three

Summer looked her grandmother over from head to toe. Martha Creswell looked healthy and happy. Memaw had always been on the voluptuous side, but now she fairly glowed with energy and good health.

"Have you been taking your blood pressure medicine, Memaw?"

Martha patted her on the arm. "Of course, darling. But the doctor tells me I'm doing better than ever." Then she held up her arm like a weight lifter. "Pumping iron and water aerobics. I've lost fat and gained muscle."

Summer wondered at that, but she couldn't argue with her grandmother. Before she could pose another question, Martha pulled her along. "I see you've met Mack here." Then Martha stopped in mid-stride, causing her colorful muumuu to pool around her legs. "Oh, my. That means you know about the house."

Summer held her grandmother's arm. "Yes, I had to hear about it from *him*." She shot a scowl toward Mack. "Why didn't y'all let me know?"

Martha shook her head. "It happened kind of fast—"

Summer interrupted her with a loud hiss of breath. "I knew it. Daddy pressured y'all, didn't he?"

Martha looked confused. "Well, no, not really—"

"Summer, my little pea blossom!"

The loud voice announcing her grand-father caused Summer to whirl around and brace herself for another hug. "Papaw!"

Summer took in the Hawaiian shirt and khaki Bermuda shorts, the stark white socks and strappy leather sandals, just before her grandfather picked her up off her feet and whirled her around.

"It is so good to see you, suga'."

Her breath cut off, Summer settled back on her feet to look up at her lovable grandfather. "Papaw, what's going on here?"

He waved a hand in the air. "A luau. You hungry?"

Tears misted in Summer's eyes. That wasn't exactly what she'd meant. "Yes, but—"

"Then come on over here and let's get you a plate. We got grilled pork and chicken, and fruit and vegetables for miles—most from my garden out back—"

"You still have a garden?"

Martha piped up as they escorted Summer toward the curious crowd. "He sure does. Everyone here calls your Papaw the Garden King. He's in charge of the garden for the whole village. Came in and took over the one they had planted. Made that puny garden spring right to life."

"That's nice," Summer said, raising her eyebrows at Mack Riley's triumphant I-told-you-so smile. "I'm glad you still have that, at least."

Her grandmother stopped right before they headed into the throng of vivid floral polyester and orthopedic shoes. "Honey, we've got lots to tell you, but that can all wait until later. Right now, I want you to meet some of our friends here at Golden Vista. We just love it here."

Summer blinked back her tears. "I'm glad, Memaw."

But she wasn't so glad. She was fast going into sensory overload, her unresolved resentment at her parents ever-building inside her tired, steamed bones. Since the night she'd broken things off with Brad, she'd longed to be back here in Athens, at home, safe in the house she'd loved all her life, with the grandparents who'd taken her in without questions or judgment and given her unconditional love.

She'd suffered right along with April back in the spring, when April's father, Stuart Maxwell, had passed away, and Summer was still feeling the effects of that and her ugly breakup with Brad Parker. Uncle Stuart had always been larger than life and so much a part of Summer's world, that her grief had been overwhelming at times. But, she reminded herself as she took in the colorful decorations and the festive tiki-themed party plates and cups, her cousin April was happy now. Happy in Paris, Texas, near Reed Garrison, the man she'd always loved. They were getting married in September.

Reed, who'd always been the boy next door, would soon be April's husband. And April would be moving into his house. They had grand plans for the Big M Ranch. They were going to turn it into some sort of vacation resort, because April wanted it to be filled with happy people, and she also wanted to honor her mother by showcasing her artwork there. The Big M certainly would make a lovely, peaceful vacation spot, but even that was changing way too fast for Summer to comprehend.

Summer wanted to be happy for her cousin, but lately, she'd been in a blue fog of regret and resentment, causing even her best intentions to go sour.

Which was why she'd taken this leave of absence to drive home. She'd needed some time to think about her life. In spite of the stress of her job, she didn't like feeling bitter and resentful all the time. She wanted to be happy again.

But now she had to worry about her grandparents.

And *him,* of course.

The man who'd stepped in and bought her grandparents' home right out from under them.

She cast a glance toward Mack Riley, trying to stay unaware of his rugged, craggy good looks and his gentle, smiling gray-blue eyes. But she was very aware, because the man looked at her with all the intensity of a lone wolf out on the prowl. A wounded wolf, she decided.

How she knew this, Summer couldn't picture. But she could almost see that something inside him that drew her to him. She'd seen that look in enough hurting people in the city. And it reflected that empty, unsettled spot deep inside her own soul.

"So you met Mack?" her grandfather said, echoing her grandmother's earlier question. "A good man, this one. Salt of the earth."

"Yes, we met," Mack said, answering for both of them. "Summer wanted to see you two right away, though."

"That's so nice of you, to drive her over here, Mack," her grandmother said, her smile beaming with maternal pride and matchmaking sparks. "Wasn't that nice of him, Summer?"

Summer didn't comment. She couldn't. She felt a huge suffocating lump in her throat. Mack was right. She didn't like change. Not at all. And she certainly didn't like being put on the spot. She was spinning out of control, and she suddenly felt lost and all alone.

This was too much, all at once, out of the blue like this. She wanted to go back, way back, to her childhood. To her room on the second floor of that old house. To frilly pink curtains blowing in the wind, to the fresh smell of line-dried sheets and gardenias from her grandmother's garden beside the back door, to the secure knowledge that they'd have biscuits and gravy and fried chicken for dinner, and some sort of fresh fruit cobbler for dessert on Sunday, right after church. She wanted to go back to family picnics down by the stream, and her grandparents laughing and each holding one of her hands as they walked down the dirt lane toward the blackberry bushes and the plum trees.

But she couldn't go back.

Summer looked up as Mack came to stand beside her. "Are you okay with all of this?" he asked, his eyes gentle and seeking.

"Do I look okay?" she managed, her voice grainy and strained, her eyes burning with tears she wouldn't shed.

"You look just fine. Maybe a bit tired and travel-weary."

She let out a struggling laugh. "I am that. Travel-weary. Very travel-weary."

Martha heard her comment. "Well, you're home now, darling. You're home and you're safe."

Summer almost did cry then, but the look of sympathy in Mack Riley's eyes stopped her cold. She wouldn't have that nervous breakdown today, after all. Instead, she flared her nostrils. "Where's the beef?"

Martha pushed Summer toward three very curious women who'd been watching them. "Summer, I want you to meet Lola, Cissie and Pamela. Lola is our director here at Golden Vista. Cissie is her administrative assistant and office manager and Pamela is our activities coordinator."

"So wonderful to meet you," blond-haired Lola said, extending her hand to Summer. "Your family has done so much for Golden Vista."

"Yes," Cissie said, her short red hair glistening in the sun. "We just love your grandparents. And your parents are always so helpful when they come to visit."

"Really?" Summer asked, surprised to hear that.

"Oh, they love to cart the residents around," Pamela answered, her blue eyes twinkling. "They take them all over. Road trips, shopping excursions."

"Well, you just never know," Summer replied, amazed that her parents even bothered.

"C'mon, now," her grandfather said, tugging her toward the table full of food. "You need to eat more."

"But ain't she still as pretty as a summer day?" Martha asked, her gaze trained with glee on Mack.

Mack lifted his chin. "Is that how she got her name?"

Martha nodded. "It suits her, don't you think?"

"Perfectly," Mack said, his eyes locking with Summer's.

Summer suddenly lost her appetite.

Mack couldn't eat another bite. These fun-loving senior citizens kept filling his plate with piles of food, and he gratefully ate every morsel, maybe because he had a lot of nervous energy and eating seemed to help curb that, maybe because he couldn't stop staring at Summer Maxwell, and wondering what would happen next with this volatile, intriguing woman.

Who knew she'd be so…pretty.

Summer had the look of a leggy California blonde, but she had the brash nature of a purebred Texan. She wasn't going to take anything lightly. Especially him moving into her grandparents' house.

Mack wanted to explain things to her, but he held back. It probably wouldn't matter anyway. Once he had her settled, wherever she decided to land, he wouldn't have any excuses for seeing her again. She'd visit with her folks, get some rest, then go back to her life in New York.

He'd certainly heard all about that life from her grandparents. A loft apartment with her two cousins in Tribeca, a stressful job as a social worker at one of the toughest YWCAs in the city, a social life that went bad more than it turned out good. He still remembered Martha's words to him just last week.

"Pray for my granddaughter, Mack. Summer is hurting so much and I can't get through to her. She needs to remember to lean on the Lord, but she thinks everyone has let her down, even God. My daughter Elsie, she doesn't understand Summer the way I do. Those two are as different as night and day."

Night and day. Maybe that's how he and Summer would be, too. Two very different people forced together under awkward circumstances. She'd never forgive him for buying Jesse and Martha's house. He'd never be able to make her see that he'd needed a place to heal because he'd been let down a lot, too.

Summer found a quiet spot away from the party. Pulling out her cell phone, she checked to see if she had any messages. None. Quickly, Summer text-messaged her cousin Autumn in New York.

U won't believe. GPs in retirement home. No house. Not sure what 2 do now.

She hit Send and let out a sigh.

"What are you doing?"

Summer whirled to find Mack Riley leaning on a gazebo post, his cool gray-blue eyes trained on her.

Finding a bravado she didn't feel, Summer tossed her phone back in her tote and said, "I'm checking for messages, not that it's any of your business."

"Okay then." He turned to go, his hands up in the air.

"Wait," she said, regretting her rude nature. "I'm sorry. Look, it's just been a long day and I'm really tired."

"Want me to take you home?"

She raised her brows. "And where would that be?"

He shrugged, gave her a smile that made little flares of awareness shoot off in her system. "You have several choices."

"Really?"

"Yeah. You can go to your parents' home. You can stay here in one of the guest apartments they keep for family, or I can stay here in an apartment and…you can have the house, keeping in mind, of course, that the house is barely livable right now. But you could sleep there at least."

Summer felt as if a soft wind had slipped up on her and knocked her flat. "You'd do that for me? Give up the house, I mean?"

"Only temporarily," he said, grinning. "But, yes, if it would make you feel better, I'd be glad to do that. I go back and forth between Golden Vista and the house and sometimes spend the night there, but I'd stay away if you decided to stay at the house."

Summer thought about his offer. It was so tempting, but then, the house wouldn't be the same. Nothing was the same. Mack owned it now, for whatever reasons. She couldn't bear to stay there without her grandparents.

"I think I'll just stay here at Golden Vista for now," she said, her voice hoarse with frustration. "But…thank you for the offer."

He pushed off the post and came toward her, that predatory look in his eyes. "Want me to take you to the office, so you can get a key?"

"Sure." She wanted a long soak and a soft bed. "I'm so tired." Then she stopped. "I forgot about my car. I need to call a tow—"

"I already did that."

"You did?"

"Yeah. While you were having another slice of pineapple upside-down cake."

"I only had one slice, but it was a really big one."

"Yeah, right. You have quite an appetite."

She smiled then. "I can pack it away."

"It looks good on you."

Summer wasn't one to blush easily, but she did now. "I like to walk," she said by way of explaining herself. "I walk all over New York. Especially in Central Park."

"It's a nice park."

Surprised that he'd been there, Summer realized she knew nothing about this man who'd moved to Athens and intruded in such a big way on her life. Or rather, the life she'd left behind. "When were you in New York?"

"Years ago," he said as he looked off into the setting sun. "A lifetime ago."

"And I lived here a lifetime ago," she retorted.

"But we're both here now."

"Yes," she said. "Isn't it funny how things happen that way. You just never know—"

"No, you don't," he replied as he guided her back toward the covered walkway. "I never dreamed I'd wind up in a small Texas town, working at a retirement complex."

The warm, fuzzy feelings Summer had been experiencing turned cold and harsh. "You work *here?*"

He nodded, looked sheepish. "Maintenance man and groundskeeper. That's why I stay here sometimes. Sorry."

"Why didn't anyone tell me that?"

"Didn't seem important. Besides, you and your grandparents were too busy having a good time."

She regarded him as if he'd turned into roadkill. "So that little news flash sort of slipped your mind."

He shook his head. "I didn't think it would matter one way or another."

"You're just full of surprises, aren't you?"

"You wouldn't believe," he said, his smile open and pure. And challenging.

Summer wanted to believe. She wanted to think that Mack Riley was just a nice man who'd become friends with her grandparents. But she'd learned not to accept things at face value. Especially pretty words coming from handsome men.

Something else was up here. Something that didn't sit well with Summer. And she intended to find out what that something was.

Chapter Four

"Are you all settled in, honey?"

Summer turned from putting clothes in the white chest of drawers to answer her grandmother's question. "I think so. This is a really nice apartment."

Martha beamed her pride. "Yes, the Golden Vista is so accommodating to family members. They have two of these efficiency apartments, I think. And they keep them open to anyone who wants to come and visit. We've even got Internet hookup, so you can use that laptop thing I saw you unpacking."

Summer tried to muster up some enthusiasm as she glanced around the homey

L-shaped apartment. "I've got wireless, but that's convenient."

Martha rushed across the sitting room-kitchen combination. "What's wrong, darlin'?"

Summer never could hide anything from her shrewd grandmother. "Nothing, Memaw. I'm just tired…and all of this is a bit overwhelming, I guess."

"I told Jesse we should have called you and told you about selling the farm, but it was kind of spur of the moment. Then once we got here, well, we're always going and doing." She shrugged, shook her head.

"It doesn't matter," Summer said, finishing her unpacking with a slam of the last drawer. "I haven't exactly been faithful in the calling-home department."

Martha came to stand next to her, her arm going around Summer's shoulders as they stared at their reflections in the oval mirror over the dresser. "But we always knew you were there if we needed you."

Summer looked down at her petite grandmother, love pouring over her. "Why didn't you…call me? I mean, if you needed money or a place to live—"

"Oh, honey, we're all right, money-wise. Your grandfather, Lord love him, he saves money with a frugal vengeance. And whether you want to believe it or not, your parents have always helped us out. They just don't make a big fuss about it."

Summer scoffed, then laughed. "Oh, not like they make such a big fuss about everything else? The trips, the houses and cars, the celebrities they hang out with."

"They're not as bad as all that," Martha said, a touch of censure in her voice. "They just like to enjoy life. I do wish you'd make your peace with them."

Summer walked into the compact kitchen, then stood staring at the stark white counters and cabinets. A wistful ache pulsed through her heart. "Oh, I'd love to do that, if I ever saw them."

Her grandmother gave her a knowing, gentle look. "Didn't they visit you last time they were passing through New York?"

Summer raised her chin. "Yes, in the airport restaurant at JFK. That was a charming visit, let me tell you."

"But they did make the effort, right?"

"Right," Summer replied, her defenses up. "So I guess they should get the Parents of the Year award for that little layover?"

"No, but you could cut them some slack," Martha said, a twinkle in her eye.

"Okay, I'll try, for your sake at least," Summer retorted. "But…it's just too hard to explain."

Martha pursed her lips. "Well, I can't squeeze blood from a turnip, so let's change the subject. Tell me what brought you home for this special visit."

Summer wanted to pour out her heart to her grandmother, but the day had just been too full of surprises for that. She needed time to think, to comprehend all the things that were going on around her. She needed time to absorb all the country charm of Golden Vista. Right now, it was screaming just a bit too loudly for her to fully appreciate it.

So she turned to her grandmother, determined not to put one speck of worry on those loving shoulders. "I just wanted to see y'all, is all."

Martha came around the counter and took Summer into her arms. "Well, I'm so very thankful for that. I pray for you every day, honey. I pray for you to find love and happiness, and I pray for all of you girls to be safe up there in that big, scary city."

"Well, only two of us are left," Summer pointed out. "April is staying in Texas. We've got a September wedding to attend, Memaw."

"Oh, that's so precious," Martha said, clasping her hands together. "April and Reed belong together." Then she hugged Summer again. "I hope you find that kind of happiness one day."

Summer allowed her grandmother's sincere love to envelop her like a warm blanket. She closed her eyes and sank against the soft security of her grandmother's embrace, sending up her own thanks to the God she was so mad at right now. "I love you, Memaw."

"I know, darling. And I love you right

back." Then Martha let her go, but held onto her arms, her eyes going big. "So... what do you think about our Mack?"

"Mack Riley is a pushy, overbearing, overrated gardener," Summer wrote in an e-mail to her cousins later that night.

Well, actually he's not so overbearing, and he seems to be a good grounds-keeper, but I don't like the man. I didn't like him on sight, even though I must admit he's easy on the eye. Attractive in a rugged, outdoors kind of way. But I'm not interested. Not one bit. Even if the man did give me a ride and call a tow truck for my car. I'm not so helpless that I couldn't have handled that myself, but it was nice to have someone step up and do something thoughtful. But then, that same man now lives in my grandparents' house. And that's just not right. Never mind that Memaw and Papaw act as if they're on some sort of permanent vacation. I think they're just putting on a good show. I can't imagine that they'd actually be happy in this overblown old folks' home. I came home expecting to find everything the way I'd left it. But everything has changed so much. Too much. I don't know if I can handle this. Or Mack Riley.

Summer finished the e-mail, hitting the send button with a defiant punch to her mouse. She pushed away from the tiny kitchen desk and glanced up at the clock over the sink. It was past midnight, but she didn't think she'd be sleeping any time soon. A deep fatigue pulled at her, making her wish for a long rest.

"If I could just be in my bed at the farm," she said out loud to the quiet, efficient apartment. This little cracker box was clean and comfortable, but it didn't feel right. Nothing felt right.

Her gaze fell across the little white Bible lying on the coffee table. A wave of guilt hit her, making her look away. "I don't want to talk to You right now, Lord."

But the Bible's gold-etched cover drew Summer. She plopped down on the floral loveseat and grabbed the Bible, thumbing through it at random. The pages finally stopped at 1 Corinthians, Chapter 13. "Love is patience; love is kind; love is not envious or boastful or arrogant or rude. It does not insist on its own way; it is not irritable or resentful."

Summer closed the book, then stared down at the cover. "I guess I've messed up in that department." But then, she didn't believe in a perfect kind of love. Love only caused pain and heartache.

She got up and went to the curtained glass-paneled door that opened to a small outside patio. Maybe some fresh air would calm her frazzled nerves. Tentatively, so as not to wake up any of the old people sleeping all around her, Summer opened the door and stepped out onto the rectangular patio. Putting her hands in the pockets of her jeans, she took a deep breath and willed herself to find some of that love and peace she'd just read about.

"Nice night."

Summer jumped at hearing the deep, masculine voice a few feet away from her. Squinting, she saw him there in the moonlight. Mack Riley was sitting in a large white wooden swing underneath an arched rose trellis.

Summer's peace was shattered and frayed. Gone. "You scared me," she said, her gaze taking in the circular pavilion centered between the apartments.

"Didn't mean to do that."

"Don't you ever go home?"

"I do. But I told you, I'm renovating the house right now. It's a mess. I have an apartment here, too, remember? I stay over sometimes when I've got an early day ahead. Just until I get the house finished, though."

Great, Summer thought. She'd have to see him night and day, hovering around all over the complex. Maybe she could keep busy and avoid him. "So that line about allowing me to have the house all to myself was just for show then?"

His foot stopped pushing and the swing creaked to a halt. "What do you mean?"

"I mean, you knew you had an apartment here when you made the offer. And here I was thinking you were being so gallant."

"I told you I stay out there at the house sometimes, and here sometimes. If you'd decided to stay there, I couldn't have done that. So, yes, I was trying to be *considerate*."

She shifted then shrugged. "It doesn't matter. Forget it. I'm all unpacked here and things are just dandy. So how many apartments does this place have?"

"All told, over a hundred. That's just the first phase though."

Summer leaned against the wooden porch rail. "Well, I didn't realize there were so many senior citizens in Athens, Texas."

"They come from all around, looking for a good climate and a safe environment near the big medical centers. It's a long-term answer to retirement."

"I'm so glad you've got it all figured out."

"I'm just here to do my job."

She wondered about that, about how he'd wound up here of all places. But she'd save that for another day. "So what are you doing sitting out here in the dark?"

"Taking in the night air." He patted the

space on the swing next to him. "Want to sit with me?"

"No, I don't. I came out here to…take a breath before I go to sleep."

"Uh-huh. You couldn't sleep either, right?"

She put her hands on her hips. "And how do you know that? Were you spying on me through the windows?"

He pushed his feet against the flagstone platform underneath the swing, causing the swing to creak as it moved back and forth. "No, I most certainly wasn't. I didn't even know you were in that particular apartment."

"Yeah, right. You're the yard boy, and you did take me to the office to check in and get a key. You probably know every nook and cranny of this place."

"I wasn't spying on you," he repeated, a hint of irritation in his words. "I don't have to resort to spying to be around pretty women."

"Oh, and I guess you know lots of pretty women."

He got really quiet after that. Satisfied

that she'd shut him up, Summer stared off into the distance, the buzz of hungry mosquitoes reminding her it was summer in Texas.

"Not anymore," he finally said. "I used to know lots of women, back in Austin. But I'm on a self-imposed bachelor's hiatus right now. No women, no complications. And I'm happy as a clam about it."

"Well, that's nice. I'm glad you're so happy. So you decided to give up women for…senior citizens?"

"I like old folks, and the pay is good."

"That's wonderful, a real win-win situation. I guess somebody had to take care of all these flowers and shrubs."

"Yep. Don't you feel closer to God in a garden?"

"Not really." Summer turned to go inside, where she'd be farther away from Mack Riley.

"Hey, I don't bite."

"I'm not worried about that. I'm just tired."

"So come and sit with me. Relax and enjoy the night."

"I can't relax with you around. Don't you get it? You're not exactly on my A list."

"How can I remedy that?"

"By going away."

"I was here first."

"Then I'll go away," Summer said, her hand reaching for the door.

He was there, his hand holding hers. "Look, I'm sorry about…the farm. I lost my own grandparents when I was young, so I know it's tough seeing yours in a different place. Grandparents represent home and love and all that stuff. I hate you had to come back and find all of that gone. But…your grandparents are still right here, and anyone can see they love you."

Summer refused to look at him, refused to acknowledge the heated warmth of his hand over hers, or the sincere kindness in his words. "Well, there is no place like home, unless of course someone comes along and takes it all away."

"I didn't take anything. I received a very nice old house and some land, and gave your grandparents a chance to rest and have some fun in a good place."

"How can I ever thank you?"

"By forgiving me. By understanding that I'm not at the root of all your problems."

"No, but you're right there in the thick of things."

He dropped his hand away, but she could feel his fierce gaze on her. "How'd you get so sarcastic and cynical, anyway? Does living in New York do this to a person?"

Summer managed to open the door even though her hands were shaking. "No, but dealing with battered women does. I've seen it all, Mack. I don't believe in love or faith anymore. I've learned that I can depend only on myself."

"Well, you're doing a lousy job of that, too, if you ask me."

"I didn't ask you, but thanks so much for your compassion and understanding," she said, just before she slammed the door in his face. Then she made sure all the curtains and blinds were closed and shut. If only she could shut her mind down and close it up tight, too.

But she couldn't. So Summer lay in the crisp white sheets of the comfortable bed and thought about Mack Riley out there in that swing. And she thought about what he'd said to her. After pouting with each toss and turn, she wondered if maybe he wasn't right. Maybe she wasn't handling things so well on her own.

She punched her fluffy pillow. "And that ain't the half of it, buster." She would never tell him the whole sordid story. Summer was having a hard time dealing with all the details of that herself. Which, she imagined, is why she'd tucked tail and run home to Texas. She just couldn't face her cousins or her co-workers right now. She'd failed everyone, including all the women she'd tried so desperately to help.

"But I'm not telling you a thing, Mr. Mack Riley—Mr. Golden Vista Poster Boy, Mr. *This Old House* and *Curb Appeal* all rolled into one."

She couldn't give him the satisfaction of being right, of course. And she wasn't ready to set him straight by giving him all the intimate details of her sad life. So she slammed at her pillows and told herself she was just fine, thank you. Then she got up and checked her e-mails, pouring her troubles out to her cousins until she was exhausted and bleary-eyed.

But Mack Riley still stood out like a thorny blackberry bush in her buzzing, confused brain. And she had to wonder if there wasn't more to his story, too. That nagging inside her gut told her to keep digging, to find out what flaws lay beneath that outdoorsman appeal and lethal smile.

Everybody had secrets. Mack Riley was no exception.

Chapter Five

Summer woke up to the smell of bacon frying and coffee brewing. Her stomach growled hungrily. Rolling over, she glanced at the clock. Eight o'clock. After tossing and turning for part of the night, she'd finally fallen into a deep sleep. Stretching, she had to admit this bed was comfortable and this little apartment had wrapped her in a cozy cocoon.

Now the sun was streaming through the white blinds of her window. Time to start her day. "What now, Lord?" she asked as she rolled out of bed. "Do I go make crafts or play a mean game of Scrabble in the rec room?"

Right now, she just wanted to find that coffee.

After taking a quick shower and blow-drying her hair until it was just damp, she put on fresh jeans and some lip gloss, then headed up the carpeted hallway toward the dining room. It was crowded with a variety of senior citizens, some smiling and chatting, some sitting alone, cranky and cantankerous.

Since Summer felt like the latter group, and since she couldn't find her grandparents, she poured herself some coffee and grabbed a fiber-filled banana bran muffin, then headed to the brooding corner of the room.

"Who are you?" a white-haired man asked as she passed his table. He wore a Texas Rangers baseball cap and a big scowl.

Summer tried to smile. "I'm Summer Maxwell. I'm here visiting my grandparents."

"Who are they?"

"The Creswells—Martha and Jesse."

He nodded, then leaned forward. "Hey, wanna go out with me Saturday night?"

Shocked and appalled, Summer shook her head. "No, thanks. I might not be around that long."

He thumped his chest. "Hmph. Me neither."

Sliding as far away as she could, Summer thought maybe he was just lonely. "You always eat alone?"

"Nah. Sometimes I have family come to visit. When they can find the time, that is."

He looked sad for a minute, until the next available female came by, this one much closer to his age.

"Hey, Gladys. Wanna go out with me Saturday night?"

Gladys was carrying a wonderfully aged Louis Vuitton purse which she held very tightly to her middle. Fingering her double strand of pearls, she gave him a look that would have flattened lesser men, then huffed a breath. "I don't think so, Ralph. Especially since I heard you took out Bullah Patterson last Sunday night."

"We're just friends," Ralph insisted, waving a hand at her. "It was just a gospel sing, not a lifelong commitment."

Gladys kept on walking, her purse held to her side as if she were the Queen herself.

Ralph shrugged, bit into a piece of toast and stared ahead for the next conquest.

"I see you've met Mr. Maroney."

Summer looked up to find Mack Riley standing there with a tray full of food in his hands. Noting that he looked as fresh as a daisy in his clean jeans and faded red T-shirt, she wished she'd bothered to finish styling her hair and had applied a bit more makeup. Too late now. And why did she care anyway?

"Oh, yes. But he's more like Mr. Baloney, don't you think?"

Mack grinned and sat down without an invitation at her table. "I'll protect you, don't worry."

"I can take care of myself, thank you."

"Oh, yeah. City girl. Tough as nails. Right?"

"Something like that," Summer said, thinking she wasn't so tough at all. But she'd give it her best shot, because she also wasn't one for backing down.

"How'd you sleep?" Mack asked between bites of biscuit and gravy.

"Like a baby," she said, hoping she'd be forgiven that slight exaggeration. Then she drained her coffee. "So, what does one do around here all day?"

Mack laughed. "Me, I have plenty to do. Yards to mow and weed, flowers and shrubs to prune, trees for days."

"I get that you are very important and indispensable, but I mean, what do the… mature adults do?"

He stopped chewing, took a sip of orange juice, then chased it with coffee. "Well, your grandparents are in a spin class right now."

"Spin class?" Summer tried to picture her stoic grandfather riding a bike. "I don't get it."

Mack pointed his fork at her. "Maybe you ought to try it. Exercise is good for the soul, you know. It clears the mind, opens the spirit, releases all the toxic thoughts from your inner being."

Summer was thinking some very toxic thoughts right now. "I know what exercise does," she said, her tone a bit defensive. "I mean, I don't get my grandparents being into it."

"They can be into a lots of things now that they are officially retired."

She threw down the rest of her grainy muffin. "Oh, yes, here at Glory Acres, life is just a bowl of cherries."

He lifted a dark eyebrow. "You know, you need to adjust that attitude."

She shot him a scowl worthy of ol' Ralph over there. "And you need to back off."

"Not a morning person?"

She glared at him, those toxic thoughts clouding her mind. "You have no idea."

Mack polished off the last of his scrambled eggs. "Oh, I think I've got a pretty good idea. Maybe being here at Golden Vista will help you relax a little. You seem a bit uptight."

"I'm sure I'll find ways to let off some steam," she said, getting up with visions of messing up his perfect flowerbeds dancing in her head. "Enjoy your breakfast."

He smiled, lifted his fork to her in a salute. "Thanks for chatting with me. You've made my day."

Summer pushed past him, waving sweetly to Ralph as she walked by.

She didn't see Ralph glance over at Mack, sympathy clear in his aged eyes. "Got yourself a live one there, boy."

Mack grinned. "Don't I know it."

"Memaw, I don't know what to do with myself," Summer complained later as she sat out on the big covered verandah with her grandmother. Martha had insisted Summer join her for a mid-morning juice break while they watched Summer's grandfather toiling away at his garden down by the lake.

"Oh, don't worry about that," Martha said, patting Summer's hand. "We have lots to get done around here. In fact, I've already signed you up for a few jobs."

Summer swept her hair off her face. "Really?"

"Yes, honey. Golden Vista needs volunteers on a regular basis. There's basket-weaving, ceramics, crafts to make, trips to the malls in Tyler and Dallas, or shopping for trinkets in Athens Alley, things such as that."

"I don't do basket-weaving, Memaw." Just the thought of that gave Summer the hives. And she wouldn't dare try to keep up with the old folks at a big mall or the antique alley either. "I need something a bit more challenging and stimulating."

Her grandmother's gaze drifted off to the right, where Mack's fancy riding lawnmower purred away like a giant bumblebee buzzing by. "I can understand, suga', what with you coming from New York City. So I have a plan." Her smile was pure enchantment.

"What is your plan?" Summer asked, wary and weary all at the same time. "I can try crafts, I guess."

Too late. Martha's laughter was triumphant. "I've signed you up to help Mack plan the Village Festival."

"Excuse me?" Summer's heart started a buzz of its own. "What exactly is a Village Festival?" And why would she even want to help Mack Riley plan it?

"Oh, it's going to be so exciting," Martha said, slapping her plump hand against her leg. "It's a big arts-and-crafts show we're going to hold right here on the grounds, on the Fourth of July, for all of our families and friends. We'll show off all the things we've been working on—our baskets and ceramics, whatnots and sculptures, paintings and photographs, our handmade crafts and yard ornaments. We'll sell homemade cakes and pies, candy and cookies. And we plan to have this big cookout followed by fireworks. Lots of fireworks right over the lake down there. It's going to be such fun."

Summer could only imagine. She cringed, but turned it into a smile for her grandmother's sake. "But, Memaw, you only just moved here. How do you know this will be fun? It might be a tremendous undertaking."

Martha nodded in agreement, her ladybug earrings swinging back and forth. "Oh, it is a big undertaking. That's why I'm on the planning committee, and that's why I think you'd be perfect to help get things organized and in order. This festival should keep you very occupied."

Summer sank into her rocking chair, full of panic and fear. She didn't know which would be worse, sitting here in a rocking chair all summer, or planning a huge event with that man out there on the riding lawnmower. "I don't think—"

"Don't worry about it right now, sweetie," Martha said, her smile still intact. "Today, we play. Tomorrow we work."

How many times had Summer heard her dear grandmother say that very thing when Summer was growing up on the farm? There was always work to do, but Martha had managed to make everything an adventure and a challenge. Her grandmother had also instinctively known when it was time to stop and have a little fun. Memaw used to say that there was a time for every season, a time for everything under the sun, straight out of Ecclesiastes. Feeling contrite and a bit sad, Summer glanced over at her grandmother.

And for the first time, she realized that Martha had grown old.

"What's wrong, Summer?" Martha asked,

concern etched in the wrinkles of her porcelain skin.

Summer jumped up to hug her grandmother. "Nothing. I'm just glad to be home."

Martha hugged her tight. "I'm glad you're here, honey. And I'm sorry about the house and the farm."

Summer sat down on the cool tiled verandah floor, next to her grandmother's chair. "I'll be okay. I just needed to see you and Papaw. I guess it doesn't matter where we meet up, as long as you're both safe and sound."

"We are that," Martha said, holding Summer's hand in hers. "We're doing just fine."

"Promise me something," Summer said, looking out over the grounds, her eyes drawn to the man on the lawnmower.

"Of course, darling."

"Promise me you'll both be around for a very long time."

Martha's chuckle didn't seem so sure. "Well, honey, I plan on trying to stick around for many more years, but, Summer, you have to accept that when the Lord calls me home, I aim on going."

"Don't talk like that," Summer said, tears pricking her eyes. "I don't want to think about that time."

"Oh, Summer, death is a part of life," Martha replied, her own voice husky and soft. "But you have to remember that God will bring us together again one day in heaven. And honey, in heaven, there are no regrets, no sadness. There is nothing but joy up there."

"I don't want to let y'all go," Summer replied, stubborn as she glared defiantly up at the blanket of clouds moving over the sky. "And I can't picture that kind of joy. Joy always comes with a heavy price, if you ask me."

Martha lifted Summer's chin with one hand. "Don't talk like that, now. Haven't you had joy in your life? Haven't you felt God's love inside yourself?"

Summer thought about the bad relationship she'd just left behind. There had been a certain kind of joy at the beginning, but that had quickly dimmed under a weight of doubt and denial. And what she'd believed to be love had only been a sick kind of enabling, a sure sign of a weakness she'd never dreamed she possessed.

"I don't think I have," Summer replied. "I know I love you and Papaw. That's a perfect love, because I know you've always loved me back, in spite of my flaws."

Martha smiled down at her. "Well, that's exactly the kind of love God feels for us, Summer. He loves us in spite of our flaws."

Summer had to wonder about that. If God loved her so much, why couldn't her own parents be proud of her? Why had they left her so many times for something better just over the horizon? When she thought back over her childhood, she saw her grandmother sitting in the school auditorium, watching her in the school play. Or she saw her grandfather sitting in his pickup truck, waiting for her to finish dance lessons or cheerleading practice.

But she couldn't remember a time her own parents had bothered to be there. For anything important in her life.

She only remembered the excuses, the

cards sent days after an event was over, probably sent only because her grandmother had reminded her parents to begin with.

They'd missed out on so much. She'd missed them, all of her life. Why had they left her? What was so wrong with her that they didn't want to be a part of her life?

Shaking her head, Summer wondered if maybe it wasn't time to stop being bitter. Her bitterness had caused her to fall for Brad Parker, because she didn't see that she was worthy of a better man. Brad had honed in on that bitterness to use her, to taunt her, to have control over her. What a fine example she'd been to all the women she'd tried to help. Her shame dimmed the warmth of the sun, made this beautiful day dark and dreary. Summer lifted her face to the sun and wished she could find some of its warmth down in her soul. Maybe that was the reason she'd come home. To find some warmth again.

But not if she kept obsessing about the past and her mistakes.

"You're mighty quiet down there," Martha said, her fingers playing through Summer's long hair.

Summer turned to smile her first real smile since she'd come home. "I'm okay, Memaw. I'm going to get past the past."

"I like that attitude," Martha replied. "How do you plan on doing that?"

"Several ways," Summer said, hopping up to brush off her jeans. "I'll start with trying to make my peace with God. And… I reckon I can help you plan that festival. I need to stay busy."

Martha lifted out of her rocking chair, her grin as wide and beautiful as the Texas sky to the west. "That is the best news. We're going to have so much fun, honey. It will just be a big ol' blast."

Summer doubted that, but being here with her grandparents was the best way to heal her wounds. The recent ones, and the ones that had been festering for most of her life.

That is, if she could just avoid getting too close to Mack Riley. She'd lighten up on the grudges and the old hurts, but she wouldn't open up her heart again for a man.

Not in this season. And not for many seasons to come.

Chapter Six

Mack had seen the two women sitting under the shade of the verandah this morning. What a pretty, heartwarming picture they made, Summer with her long hair, curled up like a child at her grandmother's feet. He could almost sense that little lost girl inside her.

He'd been lost like that once, lost inside self-doubt and too many temptations. But now he was safe here in Athens. He loved the simplicity of his life here, loved his job at Golden Vista. He enjoyed renovating the old farmhouse and hoped to turn the place into a good, solid home. The work both there and at the retirement complex was hard and constant, his duties changing with the season, his need to help out being fulfilled each time one of the residents called him to change a lightbulb, or find a lost cat. He stayed busy, but he no longer experienced the stress and burnout he'd felt back in Austin.

That seemed like a lifetime ago, his job as a landscaping architect for large corporations. He'd moved up the ranks from working exclusively for one firm to becoming his own boss. He'd been a self-made man with a whole team of people working under his supervision. He'd made good money and moved in some very elite circles. But he'd lost his soul somewhere along the way. And after years of struggling and fighting and trying to please everyone else, he'd lost the only woman he'd ever loved, too. That she didn't love him back enough still sat sour and flat against Mack's gut.

So he could feel for Summer Maxwell. He could sympathize with her need to find home and hearth again, after experiencing a crisis of sorts in her busy life. He'd left the illusion of finding a family of his own behind, while she seemed to be running back toward it. But Mack couldn't deny the love he felt for his "adopted" family of senior citizens. They'd taken him under their wings and nurtured him until he'd become a part of their little community. He wanted it to stay that way.

And he hoped with all his heart that Summer Maxwell wouldn't change the status quo. He did not need the complication of having to deal with an overbearing, hostile female in his life. Even one with long blond hair and big beautiful blue eyes.

Mack finished putting away his gardening tools, then strolled down to the vegetable garden he'd helped Jesse rework. Summer's grandfather was out there as usual, toiling away, a straw hat on his near-bald head.

"You still at it, old man?"

Jesse looked up with a grin. "I can outlast you any time, *young* man."

Mack put his hands on his hips and eyed the lush okra and squash, the butter beans and tomatoes, the black-eyed peas, the bushes thick with blackberries and blueberries. There was a whole variety of vegetables and fruits here, enough to feed all the residents and then some. Just thinking of a dish full of hot blackberry cobbler with ice cream made Mack glad he'd moved here.

"You've done a fine job, Mr. Jesse."

Jesse stopped to mop his brow with his white handkerchief. "It ain't bad, if I do say so myself. But I can't take all the credit. Everyone's helped out." He waved a hand down one of the neat, long rows. "And I couldn't help but notice somebody's been hoeing weeds for me. That person wouldn't happen to be you, now would it?"

Mack grinned, shook his head. "I'm not talking."

"That's what I thought," Jesse said as he gathered up his own tools and called it quits for the day. "I appreciate it, son. My old back ain't as strong as it used to be."

"No big deal," Mack replied as they walked together toward the building. "I had some extra time on my hands."

"How's the house coming?" Jesse asked, trepidation and wonder mixed in his voice.

"I'm taking it a room at a time. New wallpaper, paint. I'm putting in all new appliances—" Mack stopped at the far-away look in Jesse's eyes. "I'm sorry. I shouldn't go on and on like that about the house you lived in for so many years."

Jesse held up a hand. "Now, Mack, we sold the house to you. It's yours now, even if I do miss the place now and again."

Mack stood back as Jesse carefully cleaned his tools then put them inside the storage area next to Mack's. Mack locked up the shed, then turned to Jesse. "Are you happy here, Mr. Jesse?"

Jesse puffed out his chest. "Sure I am, son."

"I mean really happy?" Mack asked.

"I guess I'd probably be happier back at that old farmhouse, but life changes just like the wind. I have to go with the flow and hope God has something better just around the bend for me."

"How do you know whether you made the right decision?"

Jesse stared over at Mack, his aged brown eyes filled with a knowing light. "I pray, son. Each and every day. I pray for the Lord's guidance."

Mack nodded. "I do that, too, but sometimes I still have doubts. And I guess, what with your granddaughter showing up all in a huff—"

"Is that what this is about?" Jesse asked with a chuckle. "You're worried about Summer?"

Mack raked a hand through his hair. "Well, she hasn't exactly taken a shine to me living in your house."

"*Your* house," Jesse gently reminded him. "And Mack, there's something you should know about my sweet granddaughter."

Mack was all ears. "Oh, yeah? And what's that?"

"She's a bit high-strung," Jesse said, bobbing his head and laughing softly. "Dramatic, her grandmother used to say. Everything always becomes an issue with Summer. You should have seen her in high school. She was always fighting for some cause, trying to save everything from historical buildings to lost puppies. Her grandmother and I appreciated her enthusiasm and her passion, but I tell you, sometimes we got just plain tired out from listening to her rant and rave. But we love her anyway, 'cause she has a heart about as deep as the Trinity River, and she has this wonderful capacity to love. I think that's why she went into social work. She wanted to save all the hurting people of the world."

Mack could understand what Jesse was saying. But still he worried. "And what about herself? It seems to me, from the little time I've been around her, that Summer needs to take care of herself before she can help all those other people."

Jesse put a hand on Mack's back as they reached the side door to the complex. "Well, that's probably the very reason she came back home to Athens. She's come home to rest and take care of herself. And her granny and me, we aim to help her all we can."

"She sure loves you, too, that's for

sure," Mack said, not missing the hint of a warning in Jesse's tone. "I hope she finds whatever she's looking for."

Jesse grinned again, then patted Mack on the back with a surprisingly strong force. "Oh, I think she will, son. I sure think she will at that."

Summer collapsed against the soft floral cushions of her bed, a moan escaping her lips. "I am beat."

She turned over, looked up at the pristine white of the ceiling. The ceiling fan over the bed whirled around and around in a nice, steady cadence that almost put Summer to sleep. She didn't want to move.

Her grandmother had managed to keep her busy all day long. After taking a tour of her grandparents' roomy apartment and seeing some of their antique furniture from the farm tucked here and there, Summer had obediently followed Martha out to the garden where they'd picked butter beans, peas, cucumbers and tomatoes. Then they'd taken the vegetables inside to

be washed and passed out to both residents and workers alike, with everyone
singing the praises of her grandfather's
green thumb. Along the way, Summer had
stumbled onto some interesting old people.

"This is like being at camp all year long,
Memaw," Summer had told her grandmother at dinner, which was served
promptly at five. After that, the residents
were left to their own devices for snacks
and other refreshments. They all had small
refrigerators and stoves in their apartments.

The dining hall was long and pretty,
with colorful high-backed chairs and windows on all sides to show off the thriving
flower beds and the feisty ducks and
squawking geese prancing around out on
the small private lake.

Martha had preened and smiled during
dinner, waving to friends as she described
each under her breath to Summer.

"The Butlers—she's his second wife.
They've only been married ten years, I
think both were widowed before. Five

children and seventeen grandchildren between them. They do a lot of visiting back
and forth between all the families. But
when the youngest grandkids come here,
mercy, those boys do get a bit rowdy.

"The Gaddys—old money from Tyler.
Two grown children who live far away,
spending their inheritance already, I imagine. Mrs. Gaddy has her hair done once a
week and her nails done every two
weeks—right here in the beauty parlor.
She has a poodle named Chloe."

"Y'all have a beauty shop?"

"Yes, and a spa, too. You could benefit
from a massage and facial, you know."

"And pets?"

"Yes, a lot of the residents have pets,
dear. Of course, your grandfather and I
didn't want another one after old Sawtooth
died."

Summer remembered Sawtooth. The
big tabby had gotten that name because of
his sharp teeth and his tendency to bite
anything that moved. Summer had loved
him completely, and the big cat often slept
at the end of her bed.

"I miss him," she said, remembering the day her grandfather had called a couple of years back to tell her that Sawtooth had gone on to kitty heaven.

"We do, too," Martha said, still waving to anyone who'd look up. "This is my granddaughter, Summer," she told several of the residents sitting nearby.

And so the dinner had gone, with Summer eating the tender baked chicken and steamed vegetables sitting before her, then devouring the chocolate Texas sheet cake that followed. Memaw had reminded her they'd be having blueberry pancakes for breakfast tomorrow.

A girl could get used to this, she decided.

Until she'd looked up to find Mack Riley sitting at a table with three senior women.

Flirt, she'd thought at the time. But she had to admit Mack had been a perfect gentleman, getting up to help the women with their plates, bringing them fresh glasses of tea and coffee, and always, it had seemed, managing to cast a glance her way.

Then he'd actually gotten up and come to visit their table, much to Summer's dismay.

"Mack, so good to see you," Martha said, waving him down into an empty chair. "Isn't it good to see Mack, honey?"

"Wonderful," Summer said, saluting him with her water and lemon. "Don't you ever go home?" she asked him, causing both her grandparents to lift their eyebrows in shock.

"I'm going back out to the house this weekend," he said, obviously not offended at all by her pointed question. Then he really sprang something on her. "Hey, how 'bout all three of y'all come with me on Saturday?" He looked at Summer's grandfather. "Jesse, I sure could use your advice on a couple of the construction problems I'm having, and Martha, well, I was hoping maybe you could offer me some suggestions on decorating schemes. And the blueberry bushes are bursting with fruit. I can't possibly pick all those berries by myself."

Then he'd looked at Summer, silent and

assessing. "And I'm sure you'll have a few suggestions, too, right?"

Summer rolled over on the bed now, remembering the challenging light in his eyes. "Oh, yeah, buddy, I have a few very direct suggestions, but none of them have anything to do with curtains or cushions."

Of course, her grandparents had jumped at the chance to help Mack. They were so enamored of his lethal charm, they couldn't see past the noses on their lovable faces.

"While we're there, maybe we can get a plan going for the festival, too," Martha had suggested. "Time is a wasting. We only have a few weeks."

So Summer's Saturday was already booked, thanks to Mack's thoughtfulness and her grandmother's eagerness to keep her busy. "Thank you very much," Summer said into the silence of her little apartment, raising her hand in a wave of frustration.

On the one hand, she found it incredibly sweet that Mack had thought to include her grandparents in on the renovations of what used to be their house. It would cheer them up and give them something to keep them active and needed, even if the whole plan was a bit strange.

On the other hand, she had to wonder if Mack wasn't just buttering them up to help with the transition of losing their home and having to move to Golden Vista, maybe to appease his own guilt some, too. And she still wasn't sure what his motives were toward her.

Probably wanted to torment her and aggravate her, just to pass the time away.

"Well, I can handle you, Mack Riley. I've swept the floor with men twice as ornery as you."

What about Brad? that inner voice asked, the tone inside her head accusing and taunting.

"Brad is history," Summer reminded herself, pushing back the awful memories of their last few days together. "I learned from my mistake and Brad won't ever bother me again."

But what about how Brad has undermined that bravado of yours?

She thought about all the women she'd helped over the years. Women on the run from abusive husbands and boyfriends. She'd stood up to those men, bringing her expertise and the law down on their pathetic heads. But she hadn't been able to stand up to Brad.

"I'll be okay," Summer said out loud, effectively blocking out that dark pain. Then she got up to turn on her laptop. "Time to e-mail an update to the cousins."

She opened her mail to find replies from both April at the Big M in Paris, Texas, and Autumn in New York. And—she couldn't help it—she looked for e-mail from her parents, too, only to find none there.

Had she really expected a reply from her parents, even though she'd told them she'd be coming home to Athens for a few weeks this summer?

Summer cleared her head of that particular question, then concentrated on catching up with April and Autumn.

"I miss y'all both," Autumn said in her short, precise e-mail.

I'm up to my eyeballs in work, of course. Do y'all know what's going on with my Daddy? He's been acting really strange. I hope everything is okay at the firm in Atlanta. You know Daddy will never retire, so I hope he's not working too hard. April, how are the wedding plans progressing? Summer, what's this about Mack Riley? Who is he? And how in the world did he wind up in Athens?

"Good question," Summer mumbled, grabbing a bite-sized candy bar from the lovely basket one of the residents had brought to her door earlier.

Then came April's reply to both Summer and Autumn.

Autumn, how is it there in the loft all by yourself? Or do you have your nose buried in finances to the point that you haven't even noticed we're gone? About your daddy, talk to Uncle Richard, honey. He's okay as far as I know, so I can't speak for him. But you might want to give him a call and check up on him and your mother. I can't wait to show y'all my wedding dress. It's so pretty. And I made the final choice for the flowers yesterday.

Your bridesmaid dresses are lovely, too,
of course. Satire originals—designed just
for my wedding. Summer, this Mack fellow sounds very interesting. Just be careful. You need to rest and regroup.
Autumn, call your daddy. Soon.

Summer had to laugh at the way her
cousins' messages always fluttered from
subject to subject with a stream-of-con-
sciousness flow. But she'd learned long
ago how to keep up and respond. She'd
have to e-mail April privately later to find
out why her cousin kept insisting Autumn
call Uncle Richard. Maybe April did know
what was going on in Atlanta, but was
afraid to tell Autumn. Hmm.

But, right now, she had lots to tell her
cousins about Mack.

"I'm on it," Summer typed, thinking
Mack Riley was more an annoyance than
a real distraction. An annoyance with a
charming country-boy smile and bright,
intelligent granite-colored eyes.

Remembering those eyes, Summer answered her cousins.

Mack Riley is just a man who happened to buy my grandparents' house. A man who also happens to work at the Golden Vista Retirement Village. A man who just happens to invite himself to sit down at our table each time we go into the fancy dining room. A man who just happened to invite Memaw, Papaw and me out to the house that used to be ours to help him with renovations. A man who just happens to like to sit out in the big, open verandah and swing on the pretty white wooden swing that I'm sure he probably helped build. But, enough about him. I am resting and regrouping. And I'm going to help Memaw plan a big summer festival here at the lovely acres. Just to stay busy. Oh, did I forget to mention that my partner in all of this is...Mack Riley?

Summer shook her head, signed off and wondered how many e-mails would be passing between her two cousins after they read what she'd written. She knew they'd jump to the wrong conclusion. They'd think she was actually interested in Mack Riley.

"I'm not, of course," she said as she went into the small bathroom and got ready for some television and then bed. "I'm not."

But she had to agree with her cousin Autumn on a couple of things that had been bugging Summer already.

Looking at her clean face in the mirror, Summer asked, "Who exactly is Mack Riley? And how did he wind up in Athens?"

Deciding to forgo television and do some Internet sleuthing instead, Summer poured herself a huge glass of diet soda and got busy. She knew how to find out things about people. And she really wanted to know the scoop on Mack Riley.

Chapter Seven

A few days later, Summer finished helping her grandmother fold clothes in the community laundry room. "Memaw," she said, careful to sound nonchalant, "what do you know about Mack Riley?"

Martha buttoned one of Jesse's Sunday shirts, then smoothed it on the hanger. "Well, I know he's a hard worker and that he's very good at his job." She lifted a hand toward the windows of the long airy room. "Just look at the landscaping around here. It's lovely."

Summer had to agree there. The grounds of Golden Vista were bursting with color. Even in the summer heat and humidity, Mack's gardens seemed to be thriving as the red geraniums fought to overtake the yellow marigolds and pink gerbera daisies. "He does seem to know a lot about landscaping and gardening."

"Well, yes, of course he would," Martha said with a chuckle. "He went to school at Texas A & M for that very thing. Landscape architect, I believe is his official title—or was, at least, when he was back in Austin. He worked for some big company for a few years, then he branched out on his own. I think he was very successful for a while."

Bingo. Her grandmother had unknowingly confirmed what little bit of information Summer had been able to find on the Internet. Who knew that so many Mack Rileys, or at least several variations of that name, lived and worked all over Texas? She'd narrowed her search down to the top two. And one of them had been a landscape architect in Austin, Texas.

A very successful landscape architect, from what Summer could tell. But the Web site for Riley Landscaping and Design needed updating. Nothing had been posted there in the last few months from what

Summer could tell. That had been another red flag. Why had he just up and left a lucrative business?

"How long has Mack actually been in Athens?" she asked her grandmother as they walked back to Martha's apartment to put away the few clothes they'd washed and dried.

"Oh, a few months, I reckon," Martha replied. "He was in town for interviews before the board of directors hired him to maintain the grounds here. Then of course, he bought our house and that's when we really got to know more about him." She stopped as Summer unlocked the apartment door. "Why are you so curious about Mack, honey?"

Summer concentrated on getting the key in the lock. "Oh, just wondering. It just seems strange that he'd want to settle in a small town—I mean if he had a successful business in Austin."

Martha laughed again as they entered the cool, spotless apartment. "You can be honest, Summer. I mean, Mack is the only eligible bachelor under sixty-five around here. It stands to reason you'd be interested in him."

"Only because I don't like the way he came in and took your home away," Summer retorted, denial coursing through her heart like a deer on the run. "Other than that, I really don't care."

Martha hung up the shirts and pants, then turned to Summer. "He didn't take our home, honey. We chose to sell it to him."

"After my father coerced you into moving here."

Martha pulled Summer by the hand, bringing her back into the tiny kitchen. "Sit," she ordered with a gentle voice, shoving Summer onto a swivel chair decorated with a hand-embroidered cushion.

Summer sank down, then propped her chin in her hands, elbows on the counter. "Memaw—"

"Listen to me," Martha said in that voice that Summer knew meant business. "Your father didn't force us to do anything. Honey, we're old. You have to face that. We were struggling out on the farm.

We didn't want to let things go down, so we decided the best thing we could do was to sell it and put the money in our retirement fund. Mack gave us the asking price without batting an eye. And he promised to maintain the farm and keep it going. He's even offered for us to come and visit anytime we want."

"That's so very considerate of the man," Summer said, wanting to stew over this some more. "But I don't trust him."

"You never did trust anyone very much," Martha pointed out as she poured two glasses of lemonade. "Especially your daddy."

"Well, maybe that's because he was never around when I needed him," Summer said, her hands cupping the cool glass in front of her.

Martha leaned across the counter, her gaze tender and understanding. "I don't condone how your parents have treated you, Summer. But your mother is my daughter. Elsie always wanted a life of glamour and riches. And she's had that with your father. But she also found something else with James. She loves him. With all her heart."

"Which doesn't leave much room for anyone else," Summer replied. "Even me."

"They do love you, darlin'," Martha insisted. "They just don't know how to prove that."

"Showing up would be a good start."

Martha looked down at the counter, then wiped at an invisible speck of dust. "Well, that's why I called them and asked them to come for a visit."

"You did what?"

"I told them you were here and asked them to come home."

Summer groaned as she got up to pour out the dregs of her lemonade. "I e-mailed them and never heard back, so I figured that was that."

Martha finished her drink then placed the glasses in the tiny sink. "Well, you know the thing about that high-tech stuff—it's so impersonal and distant. Calling them seems to work better for me."

"Funny, calling them never gets me any answers."

"Well, maybe you're asking the wrong questions," Martha replied. "And maybe this need to pick on Mack stems from your frustrations with your parents."

"That's silly," Summer replied, upset that she'd worried her grandmother so much that Martha felt the need to analyze her motives.

"I'm not going to push you on this," Martha said. "But if and when your parents come home, please try, try hard, honey, to mend this great rift. For my sake. For your grandfather's sake. Okay?"

Summer felt about an inch tall. "I never meant to involve y'all, Memaw."

"Honey, we're your family. Of course we're involved. Do you think I approve of how your parents have gallivanted all over the world? I've talked my head off to your mother, but she can't see that being half a parent is worse than being no parent at all. In her mind, she's done the best she could by you."

Summer saw the pain in her grandmother's eyes. "I know they were around *some* of the time, Memaw. I remember having to leave the farm and go with them each time Daddy would come home from the rodeo circuit, but after he gave that up they still traveled. I cried to stay with you and Papaw forever, but then, I also cried each time they'd up and leave me again."

Martha nodded. "They didn't want you traveling with them, so they didn't mind you staying with us some of the time."

"I would have been a burden, a hindrance," Summer said.

"No, darlin'. Your mother didn't want you exposed to that kind of nomadic lifestyle. There are a lot of things that go on on the circuit that she didn't want you to see or hear. And, she cried, too, whether you saw it or not, each time they left."

"So she was doing me a favor by leaving me?"

Martha came around the counter, her smile as soft as a down comforter. "Think about it, Summer. Wouldn't you have rather been here with us, than staying in a different hotel room each night? The rodeo isn't a pot of gold, and even though they had Maxwell money to sustain them, they still had to live in hotels most of the time. Your mother didn't want you to grow up living like that. She knew that old farm was the right place for you."

Summer felt as if a light had come on in her mind. "I never thought about it that way."

Martha nodded. "Your mother was torn between her duty to you and her love for your father."

"So she chose him over me?"

"No, she chose your safety and well-being over everything else."

"But why couldn't she just stay here with me?"

"She could have. But life out on the road is hard and full of every kind of temptation."

Summer got up to pace the small kitchen. "So she went along to keep my father straight?"

"That…and to help him, encourage him. He became very successful because of her efforts. She turned out to be a very good manager."

"And what about me?" Summer asked,

the bitterness back in full force. "How did I become successful, Memaw?"

She was about to say she'd done it on her own, her own way, but Martha held up a hand.

"You became the woman you are today because we all loved you and were willing to make sure you got a stable home life and a good education. You are blessed, Summer. You have a good, solid family backing you and you are a very intelligent woman. You should be very proud of that."

Summer didn't feel so proud. Not wanting to bring her grandmother any more stress, she could only nod. "I have been blessed. I know that. But…it's hard to think of my childhood without feeling as if…I didn't matter."

"Oh, you mattered, all right," Martha said. "You will always matter. You need to remember that."

Because she was feeling so low, Summer made a confession to her grandmother. "I did a google on Mack Riley, Memaw."

Martha looked shocked. "You did what?"

Summer laughed then, some of the tension flowing out of her. "Oh, that means I did an Internet search on him."

"My, my," Martha said, slapping a hand to her chest. "You almost gave me a heart attack, child. I thought—"

"You don't need to worry about that sort of thing," Summer assured her. "I just want to know the facts on the man. Nothing more."

"Oh, all right," Martha said, doubt evident in her eyes. "Me, I know everything I need to know about Mack. He's a good Christian man and he works hard each and every day. He'd make someone a very fine husband." Her eyes glowed with possibilities.

"Oh, no," Summer said, backing away, her hands up in the air. "Don't even go there, Memaw. I'm not interested in being paired off with Mack Riley."

"Whatever you say, darlin'," Martha said, her smile prim and proper. "Now, how 'bout we head to that watercolor workshop? I might just paint me a picture full of bluebonnets and Indian paintbrush."

"Oh, you're painting a picture, all right," Summer said as she followed her grandmother to the recreation room at the other end of the building. "But if you try to throw Mack and me together, it won't be a pretty picture."

Martha smiled and kept walking. "You never know, honey, what God has in store for us."

Summer knew. She knew God wasn't interested in helping her seek any kind of happiness or perfect love. She'd seen too much heartache to believe in that kind of faith.

And lately, she'd felt too much of her own brand of heartache to slip up and fall for the first man who just happened by the minute she'd entered East Texas.

Back in New York, Autumn Maxwell read Summer's last e-mail, then immediately sent her own message to April back at the Big M.

What's up with this? I think she's interested. She's sure making a big fuss out of trying to convince us she's not interested. But maybe this is a good kind of distraction for Summer. Or maybe not. It wouldn't do for her to fall for another man so soon after Brad. Especially a man she's not so sure about. Anyway, I'm worried about her. And I'm lonely. I miss both of you. Work has kept me busy, busy, but something's going on there that I'm not so sure about and nobody's talking. I keep hearing gossip about budget cuts and downsizing. But I don't have time to worry about that now. And in the meantime, my daddy is still acting strange. I think he's up to something, but he won't tell me what. April, do you know anything I should know? As usual, I'll be working late into the night. How this company expects anyone left in the firm to function if they do lay people off is beyond me.

Tell me something good, April. Talk to me about planning your wedding with the man you love. What's that like? And in the meantime, I think we need to say special prayers for Summer. She's hurting so much, she can't even begin to heal. A lot of long-held suffering going on there.

Well, got to go. The ledgers and spread-sheets on my computer screen are calling me back to work.

Back at the Big M, April Maxwell read her cousin's e-mail, then sat back in her chair to stare at the screen. "I need to call Uncle Richard."

April knew what her uncle was doing, but she wasn't going to be the one to tell Autumn. Uncle Richard had retired from running his own financial firm in Atlanta, Texas. And he'd hired a man from Louisi-ana to take over. Without telling Autumn.

"He promised me he'd tell her," April said into the night. Wondering how to han-dle this, she decided she'd call Uncle Richard and remind him to talk to Au-tumn. Her cousin would be fit to be tied when she found out that her daddy had hired someone else to run the firm with-out even asking Autumn to come home and take over. His reasoning was that Au-tumn was happy in New York and he didn't want to force her to give up her life there. But he at least needed to let Autumn decide that for herself, didn't he?

"I'll go talk to Reed," April decided. Reed would understand her dilemma and give her sound advice, just as he always did. And besides, he was going to be her husband in a little over a month—any excuse to see him and be with him until then was good. April smiled, hugged herself, then did a little jig of joy. In spite of all the work she'd had to do to get things here in order after her father's death, and the many tasks required to put together her wedding, April was happy now. Finally. She missed her parents desperately, but she had Reed. They would make a new family here on the land they both loved. She had faith in that possibility.

I just wish Summer and Autumn could feel this kind of joy, she thought. *Please, Lord, let them find their own kind of happiness.*

Mack knew he should get back to work, but the letter he'd received this morning had stopped him in midstride. Somehow, Belinda had tracked him down. And she was asking to see him again.

Mack stood staring down at the white ducks floating near the shore of the small oval-shaped lake. His history with Belinda went back many years. They'd met in college and things had progressed from there. He'd worked for her father a short time after graduating from college, but even that relationship had soured with one of Belinda's whims, and Mack had lost his job. He'd gone out on his own and worked hard to make a name for himself, until Belinda had come back into his life, apparently for revenge since she'd ruined him for good this time. Which was why he'd finally left Austin to start over.

There were so many memories, good and bad. Belinda liked to move in and out of his life, mad one day and glad the next. She also liked to keep him on standby, in case her other relationships didn't pan out. Which they never did, of course. But this time…this time he didn't feel that tug on his heart, that quickening that he usually felt whenever she decided she was ready to take him back.

Mack didn't want Belinda Lewis back in his life. Ever again.

Remembering the last time he'd talked to Belinda, he leaned his head against the warm bark of an ancient live oak, closing his eyes as he sent up prayers for restraint and self-control. *Dear Lord,* he thought, *don't let me cave. Don't let me go back into that roller coaster of a relationship.*

Mack knew just seeing Belinda again might cause him to have a lapse in judgment. So he had to be very careful when he called her. He had to make her see that he wasn't interested. Maybe he should just not call at all. Maybe he'd just ignore her letter. Letting out a long sigh, Mack batted his forehead against the tree.

"Doesn't that hurt?"

He looked up, sheepish and embarrassed, to find Summer standing there staring at him. She looked as fresh as the flowers all around her in her floral shirt and jeans.

"Are you into self-mutilation?"

"No," Mack said, thinking he probably did look pretty strange standing here banging his head against an oak tree. "Just had a rough day."

"Is that your way of waking up your brain cells?"

Her sharp-edged wit woke him up more than any tree ever could. "My brain cells are just fine, thank you. I was having what I thought was a quiet moment."

She sashayed up underneath the shady canopy of the tree, her eyes gleaming. "Around here? You've got to be kidding. With emergency call buttons going off at all hours, and missing wheelchairs, and food fights in the dining room between women bickering over Mr. Maroney, there are no quiet moments. And don't get me started on water aerobics and strength-training classes."

Mack smiled in spite of his worries. "You do have a point." He shrugged, glancing toward the complex up on the hill. "Did…did you need something?"

"No, nothing," Summer replied, her gaze scanning his face. "I just decided to come feed the ducks and geese." She held out a bag. "Old bread from the kitchen. I get all the fun chores, don't you know."

Mack laughed. "I guess you're bored beyond belief, staying in an old folks' home."

"It ain't Manhattan," she retorted as she reached inside the bag and pulled out some bread. "Here." She offered him a slice. "You can help."

"Gee, think my brain cells can handle it?"

She gave him a look that said no, but then she grinned. "It's all in the wrist, I think."

Mack broke up the bread and threw it down on the edge of the shore. The ducks immediately started squawking and quacking as they hurried to get their dinner. Two big white geese soon followed. "Careful," he told Summer over his shoulder. "Some of them are downright mean."

"I can handle the little duckies," Summer replied, laughing as a fat white mama duck waddled up to her. The ducks were docile, but one of the geese decided he wanted the whole loaf of bread.

Backing up, Summer kept laughing, the

sound echoing out over the still countryside like a sweet melody from an old song.
"Hey, slow down there, goosey-goose."

Mack stood watching her as the goose
advanced. Summer's laughter was refresh-
ing and beautiful. But then, he realized as
he held the bread in his hand, *she* was
beautiful. Her eyes were big and beguiling. Her hair shone like golden wheat at
sunset. Mack groaned inwardly, thinking
he'd gone all soft and poetic, just watching the woman. But he couldn't stop
watching her.

Until the big goose flapped his wings
and started seriously chasing Summer.

"Oh!" Summer looked over at Mack as
she rushed by. "Hey, do something. I'm
being attacked."

Mack shook his head, his own laughter
relieving some of the tension he'd felt
since receiving Belinda's letter. "I tried to
warn you."

Suddenly, Summer was surrounded by
quacking, hungry geese, ducks and ducklings. Throwing up her hands, she quickly
tossed Mack another slice of bread. "Try
to head them off."

"I'm enjoying this too much," he admitted as he tossed bread back toward the lake to create a trail for the chaotic creatures.

Summer did the same, finally throwing whole chunks of bread as she lured the big goose back to the tidbits. "Maybe we should make a run for it before they eat all of this."

Mack grabbed her hand and urged her toward the building. "Hurry."

They stopped at the verandah, laughing as they tried to catch their breaths. Summer looked down at their joined hands, then looked back up at Mack, her eyes shining with mirth. "I've never been rescued from ducks and geese before."

Mack looked back at her and realized he'd made a fatal mistake. He shouldn't have taken her by the hand, because now he didn't want to let go. Ever.

So he just stood there and slowly, ever so slightly, opened the door to his heart.

To let her in.

Chapter Eight

"There you two are."

"Papaw, hi!" Summer turned from staring at Mack to find her grandfather peeking around the corner of the building. Embarrassed, she stepped away from Mack, her hands flying to her hair as she took a breath, then straightened her long locks. Mack looked away, but not before she caught the expression in his eyes that told her he'd enjoyed holding her hand.

And she'd enjoyed holding his hand right back.

"Papaw, what's up?" She tried to sound cheery and innocent, but her grandfather's shrewd gaze seemed to sum up the situation with an acute accuracy.

"You two kids okay?"

"We're fine, Jesse," Mack said, giving Summer a look that told her they weren't finished. "Isn't it about supper time?"

"That's why I came looking," Jesse said, holding out his arm to Summer. "Your grandmother wants both of you to eat at our table."

"Together?" Summer and Mack both said at the same time.

Summer didn't miss the fear in Mack's one-worded question. She felt that same fear tripping a fluttery path right through her stomach. She wasn't sure if she actually could eat.

"I figure together is better than apart," Jesse said, giving them a curious stare. "It would be kind of dumb for each of us to sit at a separate table, don't you think?"

Summer finally smiled at her grandfather's humor. "Of course I want to eat with y'all. I just thought that Mack—"

"Mack wants to eat with us, too, right, Mack?"

Mack glanced at Summer, his expression full of questions. "I'd like to, yes. That is, if Summer doesn't mind."

"I don't mind," Summer said, thinking it would be rude to refuse. Thinking with her grandparents between them, they shouldn't get into too much trouble. Trying to lighten things, she added, "That way, dear Mr. Maroney will see that I'm not available to sit with him."

Jesse guffawed at that. "Oh, don't worry about Ralph, honey. He only has eyes for Gladys Hanes. But that woman has her nose so high in the air, I'm sure she gets cloud dust stuck in her nostrils."

Summer smiled over at Mack, comfortable now that her formidable grandfather was between them. Not sure what had just happened underneath the verandah, she pushed the warm sensations coursing through her system out of her mind. For now. Better to talk about Mr. Maroney's interesting love life than to try and analyze her own reaction to Mack Riley. "Why isn't Gladys friendly to Mr. Maroney?"

"She likes to play hard to get," Jesse explained. "She's got a bank full of money—thinks every man here is only interested in her checkbook."

Mack nodded at that. "Well, maybe we need to show her that Mr. Maroney means business. He's been pining for her for a long time, from what I've heard."

"Got an idea?" Jesse asked as they entered the cool dining room.

Mack winked, smiled. Caused Summer's heart to lurch and skip. "Flowers always work for me."

She could only imagine what kind of romantic notions this man would have. And she couldn't help but wonder what it would be like to have a romantic interlude with Mack Riley. Or to receive pretty flowers from him.

"There y'all are," her grandmother called from her table in the corner by the windows. "Hurry up now. Roast beef and mashed potatoes, Jesse. Your favorite."

"And strawberry pie for dessert," Mack said as he helped Summer with her chair. "How are you, Miss Martha?"

"I'm great. Right as rain," Martha replied, clearly tickled that Summer was with Mack. "Just sit right down and let's wait for grace. The food's getting cold."

Summer watched as the multitude of old folks headed into the dining room, some using the wall railings for support, some sporting fancy walkers or wheelchairs. She wondered how it felt to grow old. Her uncle's death had her thinking about things like that a lot lately. Maybe that was why she'd felt the need to come home just to make sure her grandparents were safe and sound.

And they were, whether she liked these new developments or not. They were still in love and still happy.

Then she looked over at Mack's gray-blue hued eyes and wondered how it would feel to grow old with someone you truly loved. She looked from his keen gaze to her grandmother's loving face. Martha smiled over at Jesse, her eyes bright with tenderness. Summer's heart swelled at that display of love. She'd seen so much violence, so much hurt with the women she'd dealt with back in New York, it was endearing to actually witness true, abiding love. She thought of Brad and how he'd treated her, and then she wondered if she even deserved that kind of love.

"What's wrong?" Mack asked after one of the residents had said grace.

Summer hadn't realized her feelings were showing on her face, but Mack had certainly noticed. "Nothing," she answered. "I was…just thinking about my grandparents." She looked over at Jesse. "I'm so glad you two still have each other, Papaw."

"Me, too," Jesse said, his fork in the air. He glanced over at his wife. "And Martha is still as pretty as the day we met."

"How did you two meet?" Mack asked, his eyes on Summer.

Martha put down her dinner roll. "Oh, I was walking home from gathering eggs."

"Gathering eggs?"

She nodded, buttered her roll. "Times were tough back then. Our neighbor shared her eggs with my big family. Two brothers and a sister, me being the baby. Anyway, my mama had sent me to fetch eggs—"

"And I came barreling around the curve in the road," Jesse interjected, a grin on his face. "Driving an old International pickup."

"Scared me so bad, I dropped my basket of eggs."

"Eggs went everywhere," Jesse said. Then he leaned forward. "But, son, to tell you the truth, I don't remember anything about any eggs. I couldn't take my eyes off her pretty face."

Mack took a long drink of iced tea, then put his glass down, his gaze moving over Summer's face. "I think I can understand that concept, sir."

Jesse's grin grew even wider. "I just reckon you can at that."

"That's a nice story," Mack replied. "I hope one day I'll find someone like that."

"You just might," Martha said, mashed potatoes on her fork and a gleam of hope in her eyes.

Summer thought it was mighty warm in this dining room, but then most old folks stayed cold. Maybe they had the air-conditioning set on a toasty temperature. Or maybe she was just having a really strange reaction to the man sitting across from her. The man who kept searching her face with those incredible gray eyes.

Wanting to break the electric hum she felt coursing through her system, she said, "It seems all we do around here is eat."

"Yeah, we like it that way," Jesse replied, rubbing his stomach. "Kinda spoils a man. This food is almost as good as your grandmother's cooking."

"Eat, sleep and be merry," Martha chimed in, her tea clinking with fresh ice. "Of course, we have lots to keep us busy, too." Then she clanked her knife against her plate. "How are the plans for the festival coming, by the way?"

"Haven't worked on that," Mack said.

"Still in the thinking stages," Summer said at about the same time.

Martha looked from one to the other, surprise registering on her face. "Well, what's the holdup?"

"More bread?" Mack asked as he passed the basket to Summer, clearly uncomfortable with this subject.

"Thanks," she managed to reply, her

fingers just brushing his. His skin felt as warm as the hot buttered rolls.

"Haven't y'all even had a chance to discuss the festival?" Martha asked, her tone all innocence.

"No," Summer and Mack said at the same time.

We've got to stop doing that, Summer thought. She didn't want everyone to get the wrong idea about them.

"We could do that right after dinner," Jesse suggested. "I know we were planning on organizing this bash when we go out to the farm this weekend, but why wait? We don't want to spend all day out there hashing out the details, right?"

"Good idea," Martha said, patting her husband on the cheek. "You two could come back to our apartment."

Mack eyed Summer. "What do you want to do?"

She wanted to run out of here as fast as she could, but that wouldn't look right. "I guess it wouldn't hurt to get a plan into action."

"Okay, then." Jesse clapped his hands

together in glee. "Me, I've got a plan of action that involves this piece of pie."

Summer had to laugh at her grandfather's antics. And she had to admit it felt good, sitting here having a quiet dinner with her grandparents and Mack.

It felt so right. Too right.

Which could only mean it was all wrong.

"No, no, I think that's all wrong."

Summer got up to find more paper, her arms slicing through the air.

"So…we don't want a pony ride at the festival?"

Mack watched as she paced the confines of her grandparents' apartment, watched and wondered how such a high-strung woman could possibly ever sit still.

"I'm not saying we can't have ponies," she replied, her voice low since her grandparents had headed off to bed about an hour ago. "I'm just saying that I don't think it would be wise to put the ponies right smack in the middle of the yard. You know how ponies are—they'll trample the grass and mess up things."

Mack nodded, winced. "Oh, right. I guess that wouldn't be so smart. We could put the ponies down by the lake, on that level bit of ground away from the buildings."

She nodded as she brought him another cup of coffee. "And downwind."

"Okay, so far we've agreed to a dunking booth, a cake walk, a candy booth and activity booth for the kids, and face painting."

Summer sank back down on the floral loveseat across from the matching chair where Mack sat. "Plus the arts-and-crafts displays from all the residents. In spite of our many disagreements, we've accomplished a lot."

"We only had two really heated arguments."

"Hey, I don't care what you say, I don't think balloon darts are a good idea with so many residents around with cataracts and bifocals."

"I guess that would be asking for trouble. No sharp instruments for the residents, then." He tugged at his hair. "And I guess the sack race was a bad idea, unless we can figure out how to put sacks around walkers."

She laughed, tossed down her pen. Made him swallow and take in a deep breath. He wished she wasn't so attractive. He wished he could keep his eyes off her.

She looked over at him. "So what did you and Papaw decide about Mr. Maroney?"

"Oh, that." Glad to be on a safe subject, Mack gave her a sideways look. "We're going to suggest he sends Miss Gladys some flowers, as I said earlier. Something simple, but effective."

Summer sat up in her chair, a teasing light in her eyes. "What kind of flowers do you send to women, Mack?"

Mack had to swallow again. "I like all kinds of flowers, but…it would depend on the woman, of course."

"Of course."

She wasn't making this easy. But then, he had a feeling that Summer wasn't the kind of woman to make anything easy. High maintenance.

She kicked at his shin with her sandaled foot. "So what kind of flowers would you send to me? I mean, if we didn't have this…problem of you taking over my grandparents' house…and if I actually liked you."

"Thanks, I think." He mulled it over, squinted for a couple of seconds, then said, "I'd send you forget-me-nots."

"Oh." That seemed to slow her down, make her stop and think. She stared at him for a long time. "Why?"

"I think the name says it all. I wouldn't want you to forget me, ever. And I know I'll never forget you."

"Oh." She glanced at the clock, got up, back at full throttle. "Look how late it is. I'd better get back to my apartment. Lots to do tomorrow—paper angels to make, lace doilies to knit. You know, that sort of thing. And I really want to visit the gift shop. I've heard the art and jewelry in there is very good and reasonably priced."

"Okay, I get it," Mack said. "Time to

go." He started clearing away their cookies and coffee. "Let me clean up these dishes and I'll walk you back to your apartment."

"You don't have to do that."

"No, but I want to do that."

"I know the way. Second door to the right and straight on till I reach number 220."

"I'm right around the corner, so I'm going that way anyway."

"Oh, okay then."

Mack grinned as he made sure everything was back in place and all the lights turned off. He checked the door to make sure it would lock behind them. "Your grandparents must have really been tired tonight."

"They did seem to beat a hasty retreat."

They walked silently down the carpeted hallways until they reached Summer's door. He could smell the citrus fragrance of her shampoo. "I'll get our ideas typed up."

"I can do that," she said, taking the notes from him.

"I don't mind."

"I said I'd do it."

"Okay, okay." He backed away, sure that she wanted him gone. "Guess I'll see you tomorrow."

"I might be busy."

"Okay, well, if I run into you—"

"You know this can't possibly work, don't you?"

Mack lifted his brows toward her. "I think we can pull off this festival, if you'll just quit being so bull- headed."

"I'm not talking about the festival. I'm talking about my grandparents throwing us together. I don't think it's going to work and I just want you to know that right up front."

The impact of her words hit Mack hard in the gut. "I never even considered…." He stopped, leaned a hand against the wall. "Okay, maybe I did consider what it might be like with us…you and me. But hey, I can understand if you aren't inclined toward the same thing—I mean, you and me, us—together." He stalled out and started to sweat.

"You could never understand," she said, all traces of a smile wiped from her face. "No one could ever understand. And I can't hurt my grandparents by giving them false hope."

Mack's disappointment felt like liquid heat inside his body. It burned him, but it also cleared his head. "I wouldn't want to give anyone false hope. Especially you."

"Oh, so you feel exactly the same way?"

Not sure how to respond, he asked, "What way?"

"That this is a bad idea? That we should just stick to the plan?"

"Absolutely," he replied, nodding his head while his heart bobbled and plunged. "Stick to the plan."

"Good then." She nodded, turned the key in the lock. "It's better this way—that we understand each other and keep things cool between us. I didn't come here looking for love, Mack. I'm sorry."

"Me, either," he said, meaning it, but regretting it at the same time. "No looking for love. Too much else to worry about."

She shifted, opened the door a fraction

of an inch. "I'm sorry my grandparents seem so bent on pushing us together."

"Me, too." He was sorry about a lot of things.

So he turned and walked back down the silent hallway.

And heard the slamming of her door.

Chapter Nine

Saturday morning dawned bright and beautiful, much to Summer's dismay. She was hoping it would rain so she wouldn't be forced to endure going out to the farm with her grandparents and Mack.

"Great," she said as she finished her coffee. "Sunshine. Lots and lots of sunshine." Maybe the heat would be intolerable. Maybe they wouldn't be able to stay all day.

She stood at the window, watching as Mr. Maroney clipped fresh flowers from one of Mack's many beds. With deliberate precision, the white-haired man leaned over, first sniffing at the pink roses before choosing a nice fat blossom for his

Gladys. Then he moved with stiff, stooped grace toward a cluster of orange daylilies, choosing a fluffy flower to go with the roses. Not a perfect match, but endearing all the same, Summer thought. How sweet that such a grumpy old man would go to that much trouble for the woman he obviously adored.

Summer wondered if a man would ever be that kind toward her. Then she thought of Mack again. He was kind and sweet. But he was also the source of much of her woe these days. He'd come to town and messed up the status quo.

But you weren't here to keep him from doing that.

Summer turned from the window, determined to get through this with grace and manners. But just the thought of spending this day with Mack Riley in the house that used to be her own made Summer simmer with pent-up rage. That rage pushed any kind feelings she might have had for Mack right out the window. She needed to focus on her anger, to stay true to her misgivings. She needed to remember that Mack Riley wasn't a friend. He was a foe, right up there with her no-show parents.

Then she felt guilty, even comparing him to her parents. Mack was a nice man, on the surface. And her parents were nice people, on the surface. But Summer didn't take people at surface value. There had to be something bad underneath all that charm and good-ol'-boy work ethic. Summer wished she *could* stay mad at the man, but it wasn't possible. Not after the way they'd laughed and then held hands the other night.

Of course, since then she'd explained how things had to be between them. Nothing serious. No developing, blossoming love. No good could come of it.

No good at all.

Then why did she feel so dejected this morning? And why was she dreading seeing him again? This feeling was about much more than her anger about the house and her grandparents living here at Golden Vista. Her feelings this morning were bittersweet, because she was torn between enjoying the way Mack did things to her head, and the way her heart hurt because he'd taken over what had once been a part of her life. And there was something else, some unnamed emotion that Summer couldn't pinpoint, just on the edge of her consciousness. She suspected that emotion had to do with her nonchalant, absent parents and her recent breakup with Brad. But she wasn't ready to delve too deeply into that right now.

Feeling like a teakettle about to boil over, she hurried to get dressed, throwing on a pair of old baggy olive shorts and a lightweight, sleeveless white cotton shirt. Then she headed down the hallway to her grandparents' apartment.

"Come in, honey," Martha called as Summer opened the door. "Mack and your grandfather are out back, loading up Mack's truck."

"We're all riding in that thing?"

Martha shook her head as she gathered her hat and her knitting. "Oh, no. We're going to follow y'all out there in our car, in case we get tired and need to come home early."

"I'll drive y'all," Summer said, grabbing the keys from her grandmother's hand.

"No, now," Martha said, taking the keys back with an amazingly firm grip. "You ride with Mack, keep him company."

"Memaw, I don't want to keep Mack company," Summer said, frustration coloring each word. "In fact, I'm not so sure I even want to go out to the farm."

"But we promised Mack. And I'm dying to see what he's done with the place."

Seeing the disappointment on her grandmother's face, Summer closed her eyes and prayed for patience. "Okay, but I'm warning you—don't do a number on me and leave me stranded out there with that man. You have to stop trying to match me up with Mack Riley."

Martha batted her eyes, clearly confused. "Who said anything about trying to match you two up, suga'?"

"No one has to say anything," Summer replied as she locked the door and they started out the back hallway to the parking lot. "It's pretty obvious that everyone around here thinks Mack and I should just automatically fall head over heels for each other. Even Mr. Maroney had suggested just that, and he's been busy trying to go steady with Miss Gladys. He shouldn't waste his time trying to match us up, too."

"So you're saying we should all mind our own business?"

"Something like that," Summer replied, nodding her head. "Mack and I don't need your lovable but overbearing interference."

Martha pursed her lips. "I just want you to be happy. So does Mr. Maroney. I think he wants everyone to be happy, especially since Mack's been giving him tips on how to win over Gladys. What's the harm in that?"

"There is no harm in Mr. Maroney courting Miss Gladys, but there is a lot of harm in everyone trying to throw Mack and me together."

Martha was the picture of sweet innocence and firm intensity. "Why?"

Summer stopped her grandmother at the door, lowering her voice. "I just came off a very bad relationship, Memaw. I'm not ready to take on another man right now."

Concern marring her expression, Martha looked over Summer as if searching for bruises and scars. "What happened? You never talk about that side of your life. Is there anything I can do to make you feel better?"

Summer shook her head, wincing at the memories. "Coming here has made me feel better. That's part of the reason I took this leave of absence from my job. I needed—"

"You needed to heal," Martha said, pulling Summer close. "You came home. You knew where you'd find your strength. Everyone knows Texas is one of the best spots on earth to get on with life."

Summer hugged her grandmother tightly, then leaned back. Martha had no idea just how much Summer needed to rest and heal, and yes, to get on with life. "Yes, but I can't get over Brad if I've got all these notions in my head about Mack Riley."

"You have notions?" Martha asked, obviously glad to hear that bit of news.

"I do each time you push us together,"

Summer replied, then she waved her hands in the air. "But, that's not the point. The point is—I'm not interested in Mack Riley. I'll help at the house, I'll be nice to the man, and I'll work on the festival with him. But that's it. I have to go back to New York and my job after the fourth, anyway."

"Okay, darlin'," Martha replied, a bit too quickly. "I guess we'll just have to settle for that."

"Good," Summer said, wondering if her grandmother was even listening to what she was really saying. And wondering if she was trying too hard to convince both herself and her grandmother that she didn't have feelings for Mack.

"Good," Martha echoed, a serene expression on her face.

Summer decided her grandmother wasn't very good at hiding *her* true feelings. Which meant Summer had to make it very clear to all involved that she wasn't going to fall for Mack Riley.

He wouldn't fall for her. Mack kept telling himself that as they pulled into the long drive to the farmhouse. After Belinda and her bag of tricks, Mack had made a solemn promise to be careful in the love department. He'd gone back to the strong values and firm foundation his parents had instilled in him, and he'd turned his life over to God. That meant no roller-coaster, topsy-turvy relationships. The next time he fell in love, he wanted it to be slow-paced and solid, a forever kind of perfect love, like that of his parents and of Jesse and Martha. He needed to stick to the plan, as Summer had suggested.

But he wished he knew the plan. Was he destined to spend the rest of his life alone? Mack thought about how close he and Belinda had come to marrying and having a family. He'd always thought that would happen, but Belinda had only wanted him on her terms. She wanted a man who could move in the high society she was so used to. She wanted a husband who could showcase her own beauty and help her to keep moving up the social ladder while he ca-

tered to her whims and demands. Mack
had failed miserably at being that man.

He glanced over at Summer, wondering
at the paradox of her life. She came from
a wealthy Texas family. She was considered a socialite by any standards. She'd
had privileges in her life, yet she'd turned
away from all the free handouts and set out
to make her own way in life, far away from
the traditions of Texas.

"Why'd you move to New York?" he
asked, needing to understand her.

Summer jumped in the passenger seat as
if he'd said "Boo." Pushing at a few stray
bangs, she shrugged. "My cousin April got
this idea that we needed to conquer the
Big Apple. She was running away from a
lot of bad things, so after a trip there to celebrate our graduating from college—we're
all just a couple of months apart in age—
she convinced Autumn and me to come
with her. Autumn had already graduated,
but she was working with my uncle as a
CPA in Atlanta—Texas, that is." She shook
her head. "Autumn had this ten-year

plan...which she had to modify just a tad after April got this urge."

Mack grinned at that. "So New York City beckoned?"

"Yes. April can be pretty persuasive. I think Autumn came along just to look out for April and me. And I sure was up for an adventure. I mean, my parents were never around a whole lot, and I needed to prove myself, I guess. I had my degree in social work and what better place to get down and dirty? New York is full of broken, hurting people. So, we all packed up and headed out. At first, our fathers footed the bill because they all figured we'd be back in Texas in about a month. But we slowly weaned ourselves off that and did things on our own."

"Do you enjoy your job?"

She laughed at that. Waiting for Mack to park the rickety old truck in front of the farmhouse, she shook her head. "There is no way to enjoy helping battered women. It's a tough battle. But I do enjoy the satisfaction of seeing these women start all over from scratch. It's good to see someone who's been so hopeless and full of despair turn around and find a new beginning. So, I guess I find it fulfilling, yes. But unfortunately, not all of my cases have a happy ending."

Mack saw the darkness pass through her blue eyes like clouds over water, and wondered if she took those lost causes to heart. "How do *you* deal with all of that?"

She opened her door. "Lately, not very well." Getting out, she slammed the door shut and left Mack sitting there.

He wondered what she'd seen up there in the big city. Wondered if the days and nights of so much tragedy and violence had left her frayed and damaged. Maybe that was why she was so prickly at times. He knew she was tough. He'd seen that from the beginning. But he wondered if she wasn't tender, too. Too tender to hurt. Too tender to accept false hope.

And yet, he wanted to see her hopeful. He wanted to wipe that cynicism right off her pretty face. It didn't help that she'd come home for some peace and quiet, only to find her old way of life completely changed. It didn't sit well that he'd contributed to her pain and her disappointment. Maybe today would give her some sort of closure and peace. He hoped so.

He watched her as she slowly made her way toward the house, her head down as if she couldn't bear to look at the place. He got out of the truck to follow her. "I'm glad y'all came," he said as they waited for Jesse and Martha to pull into the driveway. "I like coming out here to work on the house, but it sure gets lonely."

"I can swing a mean paintbrush," she said in response, her gaze slowly moving over the scaffolds holding up one side of the two-story house. "What's going on there?"

"Just reinforcing the structure," Mack explained. "I've had contractors out here all week working on that. They'll replace boards and shingles and paint the outside once the new windows are in."

"New windows? What's wrong with the old ones?"

"I wanted better insulation," he explained. "I plan on keeping the original design, but I also need to keep the utility bills down. Just being practical."

"Probably a good idea. I remember chilly nights here during the winter. Memaw would pile the quilts on my bed."

"That's what Jesse told me. And hot, humid summers, kind of like today."

She pushed at her hair. "I hope my grandparents don't overheat."

"I won't let that happen."

She turned to him then, her eyes devoid of any anger or doubt. "You care about them."

"Of course I do. I never knew my grandparents."

"What about your parents?"

"They still live in Austin. They're fine. I don't get back there much."

She shifted her sneakers in a mound of dirt, her thumbs hooked in her baggy pockets. "I did a search looking for information on you on the Internet."

"Oh?" He should be angry, but knowing Summer the way he did, he reckoned it fit. But he didn't have anything earth-shaking to hide or reveal. "And what did you find?"

"You owned your own company? Landscaping?"

"Are you asking me to confirm that?"

"If you want. I did it only because I was just trying to protect my grandparents."

"Makes sense, but why didn't you just ask me?"

"I'm asking now."

Mack shook his head. "You just don't trust me, do you?"

"I'm trying. I want to be angry at you, but you're too nice for that. Or so you seem."

"But you don't believe in nice?"

"I've seen nice overplayed, yeah."

Mack turned as Jesse pulled the shiny new sedan up underneath an old oak tree. "Maybe later, we can go for a walk and I'll tell you everything you need to know."

"Maybe."

Feeling as if they'd reached a truce of sorts, he headed off to unload his truck. But Mack couldn't help but wonder what Summer would do if she knew the true story of his life in Austin. And he wondered if he'd have the courage to tell her that story. Would she accept him the way he was now, or would she turn away because he'd once let a woman walk all over him to the point that he had no pride left? He wanted Summer to like him, but more than that, he wanted her to respect him.

She had to admit the old house was coming along very nicely. Summer stood in the empty living room, memories swirling around her in the dust balls that glowed in the morning sun. Everything was different now.

The long paneled room had a new coat of shiny varnish on the walls, making it seem more light and airy. The long row of windows facing the back of the house boasted double-paned insulation. That would work with the new heating and air-conditioning system. The fireplace, which had housed a horrid-looking gas heater, had been restored and polished clean, its walnut wood gleaming. The hardwood floors had been sanded and refinished. The whole room shone with a bright hope that made Summer think of a loving family and future generations of children. She had to wonder if Mack had someone special in mind to share this big house with him.

"You're bringing this place into this century, at least," she told Mack with a grudging appreciation.

He turned from clearing away some clutter. "You approve—finally?"

"I didn't say I approve. But I can certainly appreciate what you're trying to do." The easy banter between her grandparents carried from the kitchen, making Summer smile. "I just hope your two helpers don't waste more paint than they put on the walls in there."

"They're having a blast," Mack said as he tossed some old boards and wallpaper into a huge wastebasket he'd brought in from the back porch.

Summer couldn't argue with that. Her grandparents had such sweet spirits. They could roll with the punches and make anything exciting and fun. She wished she could be that way. But she'd been shifted and shaken too many times to actually see the potential in bad situations. She longed to be…settled. Just settled.

"Hey, don't look so sad," Mack said as he came walking past her, paintbrush in hand. He lifted the brand-new trim brush to her nose, tickling her with the silky fibers.

Summer crinkled her nose, then smiled. "Is that my cue to get to work?"

"You don't have to do anything," Mack retorted. "But you can keep me company upstairs."

She grabbed the brush from his hand. "No, I came to work. I need to stay busy. What are you working on?"

"The master bedroom," he said over his shoulder.

She watched as he made his way up the stairs. Did she dare go up there with him? They'd be all alone. And even though her grandparents were right downstairs, Summer felt vulnerable and exposed when she was around Mack. Maybe because of the way he'd looked at her there on the verandah the other night. Maybe because her emotions were at war right now—trying to hate him and like him at the same time.

"You coming?" Mack asked, leaning his head over the sturdy new oak railing.

Summer glanced around, couldn't find any excuses to keep her busy down here. "Yeah, I'll be right there."

She hurried up the stairs, but when she rounded the top landing she saw movement down below out of the corner of her eye. Glancing down, she just caught a glimpse of her grandparents bobbing their heads around the open arch between the kitchen and the front hallway. They quickly ducked back into the kitchen, but Summer didn't miss the keen interest in their expressions. Or the hopeful looks in their eyes.

"I must be crazy," she mumbled. "I should just walk out of here right now, right this minute."

But she didn't have anywhere to go. Her home belonged to someone else now. Her heart was battered and broken. Her spirit was depleted. She was a weary traveler who needed a place to stop and rest her head.

She looked up and saw Mack waiting

there for her, the sun shining through the windows behind him, peeling, tattered rose-hued wallpaper surrounding him. And suddenly, Summer wanted to peel back all the layers that made up Mack Riley. She wanted to explore those layers, so she could figure out what made this man tick. He seemed so sure, so secure, in his life and in his faith. He seemed like a simple man who only wanted a simple life. No hidden agendas, no past dysfunction holding him back, no pain or loss in his life.

He'd promised her he'd tell her all about himself.

Summer intended to make sure he honored that promise.

Chapter Ten

"That was a very good lunch."

Mack put down the remains of his fried chicken and potato salad, then looked over at Summer. She'd been awfully quiet during their meal out on the back porch.

"Thanks," Jesse said, grinning. "I got up at four o'clock this morning to cook this chicken."

"Hmph," Martha said, hitting him on the arm with her napkin. "You were still snoring away at four this morning. The cook at Golden Vista prepared this chicken."

"Blabbermouth," Jesse retorted, sticking out his tongue at her. "But a mighty cute blabbermouth." He winked at her, then offered her an oatmeal cookie. "Have some dessert."

"Think I might." Martha took the cookie, then stretched back in one of the old kitchen chairs Mack had set up out on the porch. "Mercy, I might need a nap. That afternoon breeze sure is pleasant."

Jesse nodded, put down his chicken leg. "Remember how we used to stretch out underneath that giant cottonwood down by the creek?"

"I remember," Martha said, a becoming blush coloring her skin. "We were so young back then. Now…I reckon I'd get stuck and you'd have to get help to get me up."

Mack laughed at their easy banter, the hole in his heart hurting with a splitting pain. He wished he could have that kind of love. He wished he knew where he'd gone wrong with Belinda. But then, he thought if he dug deeply enough, he'd find the answer to that question. And it wouldn't be pretty. She hadn't loved him enough to make a commitment, and he'd loved her way too much to see that for what it was. Nothing like getting the cart before the horse. He'd rushed headlong into that relationship, then gone against all the values he'd been taught in order to win her over. He wouldn't make that mistake again.

Putting those memories away, he glanced over at Summer. He needed to get some things cleared up between them. "Up to that walk we talked about?"

She looked up, her eyes going wide with surprise. She appeared to be lost in thought herself. Looking confused, she busied herself with throwing away their paper plates. "What about that room we left unfinished upstairs?"

They'd painted most of the master bedroom, their quiet work and easy chat a nice reprieve from all the undercurrents swirling between them. But now, Mack could see those undercurrents had returned.

"It'll be there when we get back," he said, and, thinking their *unfinished* business was more important right now, he waited for her to respond.

"Go ahead, honey," Martha said, urging Summer with a hand on her arm. "Your granddaddy and I will go in and rest—the old couch is still in the back den for me and Papaw can take the broken recliner. We'll be just fine."

"Then when y'all return, it's back to work," Jesse said. "No slackers here." He pushed off the table. "You've done a fine job on this old house, Mack. Makes me proud to know I sold it to the right man."

Mack swallowed, looked down at the floor. "Thanks, Jesse. That means a lot to me." When he looked back up, Summer was staring at him, her eyes bright with questions he wasn't so sure he could answer.

"Ready?" he asked, wondering if she'd just turn tail and run the other way.

"I guess so."

He waited until they'd cleared the porch before speaking. "Well, don't look as if you're headed for an execution."

"I'm sorry," she said, pasting a false smile on her face as she waved to her wide-eyed grandparents. "It's just hard being here like this. I'm helping you fix up the house I've always loved." She shrugged. "I'm a bit conflicted, as usual."

"You don't like the changes on the house, or you just don't like me?"

She pushed at her long hair, her eyes following the treeline along the pasture fence behind the house. The heat of summer buzzed past them in the form of bees droning and birds chirping. A pretty yellow butterfly drifted by, its wings fluttering gracefully. "I don't want to like you, Mack. But I do."

He grinned. "Score one for me, then."

"And I don't want to like this house becoming all modern and pretty, because it was beautiful to me just the way it was. But I have to agree with Papaw. You've done a great job."

Mack took that compliment in silence, admiring her direct nature. "What did you love most about this place?"

She gave him a weary look, as if that were a trick question. "My grandparents," she replied without hesitation. "I've always known I could count on them. They're solid and sure. Not like most—"

"Tell me about your parents."

She shook her head, looked out over

the rolling hills. "I don't want to talk about them."

Mack respected that, but knew she needed to talk to someone. So he tried another tactic. "My parents are the salt of the earth. We didn't have much when I was growing up, but they took care of us."

"Do you have brothers and sisters?"

"Two brothers and a sister. I'm one of the middle ones."

Her surprise turned to a pleasant smile. "What's it like, having a big family?"

He laughed at that. "Crazy at times. My two older brothers loved to harass me and my younger sister. I learned to be tough at a very early age. It was survival of the fittest."

She let her hand trail over the fence. "Funny, I learned to be tough the first time my parents left me behind."

Mack stopped and turned to face her as they reached the small creek. He put his hands on her arms, to steady her, to force her to look at him. "I can't imagine that— parents leaving a child. I've met your parents, Summer, and I don't get it. They seem like such nice, self-assured people. Really together."

"That's the key word," she said. "*Together.* They wanted to be together with each other much more than they wanted to be together with me." She shook her head. "I think they love me, but they just don't get that I...I needed to hear that, and I needed to have them here so many times, for the everyday things that a child needs."

"You're blessed that you had Jesse and Martha."

"Don't I know it. My other grandparents died when I was just a baby. I wished I could have known them. I always dreamed that they would have taken care of me, too. I could have been doubly blessed." Her smile was bittersweet. "I know I shouldn't complain, but my parents always treated me as if I were a toy. They played with me when they were in town and they put me back in my place whenever it was time to move on to something better."

"I can't imagine that," Mack replied, wishing there was something he could say to make her feel better. "But I guess parents abandon children all the time. We just don't hear about it."

"It happens," she said. "I saw it a lot in New York. And that kind of abandonment is much worse than what I ever suffered, trust me. I had my grandparents. But there are children out there who will never know their real fathers and mothers. In my line of work, it was mostly the fathers. They'd beat up their women, then either leave for good or try to hurt both mother and child. At least my parents are blissfully happy. So happy with each other, they tend to shut out the rest of the world." She shrugged. "I have this thing about fathers who abuse or abandon their own. It's just not right. So I've fought to fix it. Sometimes, I've won. Many times, I've lost."

Mack could see the hurt on her face. It made him want to protect her, to hold her and promise her that everything would be all right. And he wanted to figure out what was driving her. "Did you choose social work because of the way your parents were always dumping you?"

She drew back, her features going sharp with pain and denial. "Are you trying to analyze me, Mack?"

"No, I'm trying to understand you."

"There's nothing to understand, except that I had a wonderful set of maternal grandparents who loved me and raised me, for the most part. As I said, my other set of grandparents died when I was young, so I don't remember them at all. They left the Maxwell legacy—and all that money, while Memaw and Papaw gave me a sense of home. I suppose when you add all of that together, I grew up knowing I was blessed, but also knowing I wanted to help others— especially children. Memaw and Papaw taught me to always honor and respect my blessings by being kind to others."

"They did a good job," he said, hoping to win back some of her tentative affection. "You don't seem to be the type to let money go to your head."

"Yeah, well they tried, that's for sure. I never rebelled while living here, but I sure liked to show my angst whenever my parents returned home. That's when I'd play the money card, spending huge amounts on clothes and shoes I didn't need, just so I could go on shopping trips with my mom and then ignore her afterwards. I was trying to fill this great void, and so was she, I guess. I've been trying to fill that place for years since. Now, I'm bitter, burned out, tired, confused. I'm a walking mess. I don't know why I thought coming back here could change any of the mistakes I've made—"

She stopped, a hand flying to her mouth. "And I really don't want to talk about any of this with you."

"Because you don't want to like me or trust me, right? Because you think I just came in here and coerced your grandparents? Or is it because I bought this property through your father and you just can't cut him any slack either?"

"You don't know how I feel about my father," she retorted, her face reddening with rage.

"Oh, I think I do," he said, unwilling to back down now. He was tired of trying to justify his actions and his motives. He understood how Summer was feeling all right, but the things she'd held onto from her past had nothing to do with him. And now, just when he thought he could rest and enjoy life, God had thrown this aggravating, enticing, interesting, *conflicted* woman in his path. Was he supposed to help her or just ignore her? This very minute, he could only empathize with her. "I think I understand exactly how you feel."

She held out her hands in the air. "I thought we came out here so *you* could tell *me* all about your life. How come you've twisted it around on me?"

"I don't know. I just wanted to…to try and figure you out, I guess."

"Well, don't bother." She turned to stomp away, her long hair fluttering out behind her in waves of gold that reminded Mack of that pretty yellow butterfly they'd seen earlier.

"Hey, wait," Mack said, tugging her back around. "You really want to know why I left Austin? Why I came here to this small, sleepy town?"

She slanted her eyebrows, her head going down as she eyed him. "That would be good, for starters."

He stood, his eyes locked with hers, and decided to lay all his cards on the table. "I got burned, too, Summer. I fell for a woman straight out of college. An Austin socialite who was rich and powerful…and so beautiful.

"I went to work for her father, because she insisted I could be happy there, and because she indicated she could only be happy with me there. For years, we had this kind of sick relationship where she guided everything from the clothes I wore to the people I associated with. But it wasn't enough. I tried to convince myself that I loved her, that I'd do anything to have her as my wife. But the more she demanded, the more angry and bitter I became—with her, but mostly with myself. She'd promise me marriage, then change her mind over some incident or so-called slight. We battled back and forth and I actually left her father's company to start my own. She left me, but then when it looked like I was going to be a success, she came back, telling me how proud she was of me. I fell for her all over again and we got really close for a while. I thought maybe she really did love me. But I was wrong. She got angry over something I said, then she told me I could never support her financially, that I couldn't make her happy because I refused to accept her wealth."

He let out a breath, pinched his nose with his thumb and index finger. "I decided to show her, so I worked hard and kept on making a name for myself. She tried to get me back then, and I hate to admit this, but I gave in one last time. I gave all the way in, Summer, just to have one night with her. Then I hated myself afterwards. I had had enough. I rejected her.

"She went to her daddy and convinced him that I'd wronged her, so he decided to stick it to me real good. All the clients I'd worked so hard to acquire started backing away, one by one. And because of that, I almost lost everything. So I packed up and headed out. I had to get away. I had to start over. End of story."

She stood staring at him, her expression changing from disbelief to understanding. "I can't believe the man standing in front of me would let a woman do that to him."

He let out a laugh, both relieved and in agony that she'd immediately seen his worst flaw. "Neither can I. But then, we do strange things in the name of love, don't we?"

She flinched, as if she knew about that first-hand. "I guess we do." Then she lifted her gaze, her eyes locking with his. "Did you feel trapped when you were with her? Unable to make a decision on your own?"

Surprised that she got it, he nodded, swallowed the bile rising in his throat. "I felt as if I'd lost my soul. What I thought was love was really more about control, her need to control me, both physically and mentally. I won't be controlled again."

He thought he saw a flicker of admiration in her eyes. And maybe something else. A kind of recognition. "You feel safe here, right?"

He nodded. "Yes, I feel safe here. I feel secure now. Maybe I'm hiding out here, but at least I no longer doubt myself or my faith in God. When I left Austin, I promised Him I'd never stray again. I just want some peace and a simple life. That wasn't good enough for Belinda. It has to be enough—it is enough—for me."

He stood there, his soul bare and bruised, and wondered why he'd just spilled his guts to this woman. How could she possibly understand the disgust he'd felt for himself the last time he'd been with Belinda? How could he make Summer understand the whole ugly story about how Belinda had gotten to him one last time?

He couldn't. Some things needed to be kept inside. That part of his life was over now, and he wouldn't look back. He had asked God for forgiveness so many times, he felt raw from the wanting of it. He wouldn't count on Summer Maxwell to help appease his soul.

But when he looked into her eyes, he saw a reflection of his pain there in the blue depths. He thought he saw that understanding and peace he needed so badly.

"I'm sorry you had to hear all of that,"

he said, hoping she would at least back off now. "But I want you to understand that…I need this quiet time here, working on this house, working at Golden Vista. I need this in my life right now. And I won't apologize for being here, or for turning back to my faith to guide me. Not anymore. I just want to be settled, to be happy again."

He turned to walk past her, back to the house, but then Summer did something that surprised him and sealed his fate. She touched a hand to his face and reached up to kiss him softly on the cheek. "Then it seems we both want the same things, Mack. Imagine that."

Summer was still accepting this new turn in her heart as they rounded the lane toward the house. She had accepted that this man was becoming important to her, even though she'd only known him for about a week. Not one to rush into anything, she also accepted that this relationship would have to develop slowly and surely and firmly. Maybe they'd just become very good friends, or maybe something else would develop. But she wasn't going to hang around here forever. What then?

Then, she decided with a delicious joy, she'd have a friend to visit each time she came home to see her grandparents. That gave her a kind of sweet security as she glanced over at Mack. After their heart-wrenching confessions earlier, they'd settled under the tall cottonwood and discussed so many things, including the upcoming festivities at the retirement center. It had been nice, going back over the plans for the events with him. He really was a good man. Easy to work with, easy to look at, easy to fall for.

One day at a time, she told herself. Don't rush it. Don't count on it.

"I'm glad we got everything for the festival ironed out," Summer told him. "We can give my grandparents a full report and then next week, I'll get started on organizing things."

He smiled at her, his eyes clear of any mistrust or regret. "Are we friends yet?"

"We are," she replied, almost shy now

that she'd let him win her over. "Thanks for telling me…about your life in Austin. I know there's more—isn't there always?—but I won't press for the details. From my experience, people can't be pushed too hard to divulge the intimate details of their lives. That has to come with trust, lots of trust. I can see that Belinda hurt you, but Mack, I could never see you as being a weak man."

He blinked, turned away. "But I *was* weak. I figured you could see right through me."

"What I see is a man who's trying to get his life together, a man who works hard, tries to do the right thing, and…a man who adores my grandparents. The pros far outweigh the cons, Mack."

"Same here," he said, turning to look at her. "You think you've made mistakes. But I see you trying to find your way back from those mistakes. I guess we both are."

"So, can we agree to concentrate on the here and now, just for now?"

"Okay," he said, taking her hand in his.

"But, one day soon, I want to hear the rest of your story, too."

"Still twisting things around on me, huh?"

"Still interested in the details," he countered. Then he laughed. "As your grandmother has so graciously pointed out, we're the only two people around Golden Vista who aren't members of the American Association of Retired Persons. Guess that makes us an item of sorts."

"She told you that, too?"

"Uh, yes. I think the whole place is holding its collective breath regarding us. Even Mr. Maroney, who has a serious crush on you."

"They can keep holding their breaths," Summer replied, grinning. "Let's keep them guessing."

"Oh, I think *you* plan on keeping *me* guessing."

She stopped near the back porch. "I'll be leaving after the festival, Mack. There's no guessing about that."

"I know. But we have a few weeks until then. And since we've agreed to enjoy the here and now...."

She saw the hope in his eyes and felt that same hope reflected in her heart. "I'm in big trouble," she told him.

"I know the feeling," he replied.

Summer placed one foot on the back steps just as the door from the house burst open. She glanced up, expecting to find her overly eager grandparents grinning down on them.

But the two people she saw standing there caused Summer to grab the porch railing to steady herself.

"Summer, darlin', we were beginning to think you two had fallen in that snake-infested creek. Come on up here and let me have a look at you. Why on earth haven't you cut that hair by now?"

"My little girl's just as pretty as she was when she was a squirt running around here, don't you think, Elsie?"

"I sure do, in spite of that uncontrollable hair. Honey, it's so good to see you."

Summer shot Mack a warning look, then lifted a hand in the air. "Mack Riley, meet my parents, James and Elsie Maxwell." Then she turned to the two people staring down at them, her rage warring with her joy in full force as she confronted them. "They're just passing through, I'm sure."

Elsie came bopping down the steps, her strappy sandals clinking on the aged wood, her orange silk sheath glistening in the sunshine. "Oh, no, darlin', we've come home for a good long stay. And we want you to come and stay in our house with us, just as soon as you can get your suitcase loaded and in the car."

Chapter Eleven

Summer looked around the huge house her parents had dragged her into and wondered why she'd let them talk her into coming here. The place was overdone and tacky, a perfect example of too much of a good thing. The mansion was all silver and gold, all swirls and etchings. It was designed in a country-French style that stuck out like an amusement-park phony amid the many ranch-style houses of East Texas.

"It looks like something out of a bad horror movie," Summer said to herself, her words echoing up into the twenty-foot ceiling of the entryway. She let out a sigh, willing herself to be calm and reasonable.

At least her parents had come home. It was a start.

Her mother came tapping down the stairs, her hand moving over the wrought-iron railing as she descended like a queen about to greet her court. "Your things are all unpacked and put away, darlin'." Elsie stopped at the last step to look down on Summer. "Are you going to stand there in the hallway all day, or actually come on inside?"

Summer didn't miss the nervous laughter behind her mother's words. Elsie had always seemed a bit afraid of her only daughter. Maybe because they were so very different. Don't spook her, Summer told herself. Try to make conversation. Try to be kind.

"I'm...getting adjusted," Summer replied, trying very hard to do what her grandmother had asked in a whispered plea back at the farmhouse. Make nice.

"Well, let's go back to the den and find us something cool to drink," her mother suggested, waving her long orange-polished fingers in the air. Elsie prided herself on her impeccable manicures, which always had to match her outfits.

Summer stifled the groan she felt coming and marched up the marble-floored hallway toward the back of the big rectangular house, her mind reeling with the events of the last few hours.

After getting over the shock of seeing her parents, Summer had somehow managed to get through the impromptu tour they'd insisted on taking to look over the renovations on the farmhouse.

But not before she blurted out, "I'm not going anywhere with y'all."

"And why on earth not?" Elsie countered, her green eyes flashing with a dare. "You can't stay in that old folks' home, suga'."

"It's a retirement center," Summer purposely pointed out. "One you and Daddy convinced my grandparents to move into."

"Hey, now," James interjected, "this was a mutual decision. Your mother worried so much about her folks. It seemed like the best solution."

"Best for you, right?"

Summer stomped into the house, leaving Mack to talk to her shocked parents. But her grandmother rounded on her as she headed for the front door.

"Summer, you are missing a chance here."

Summer stopped to stare at Martha, her pulse racing. "How many chances have *they* missed over the years, Memaw? They missed my tenth birthday. They missed my high-school graduation. They missed when I was crowned Miss Athens. They missed when I went off to college, and they barely made it to that graduation. I don't think I'm missing anything, because they don't seem to care what they've missed."

"You are so wrong there," Martha replied. "Now, honey, I've never asked any more of you than you can bear. And you can bear this. Go home with your parents and spend some time with them. You're an adult now. It's time to stop this childish grudge."

"You think this is a grudge? Memaw, this is more than just a grudge. This is my life. Because of them, I—"

She stopped, unable to tell her grand-mother anything more about her life in New York, about her bad choice in men, especially Brad Parker. Summer couldn't tell anyone the shame she felt in that.

"What, honey?" Martha asked, waiting, her words almost echoing Summer's thoughts. "You know you can talk to me about anything, but you need to quit blaming your parents for everything wrong that's ever happened to you. I think you've had a pretty good life, all things considered."

Summer did feel contrite. "I never said I hated my life here, Memaw. In fact, I cherished it. You know that. It's just that… I wish I could understand—"

"Try talking to your mama, then," Martha replied.

"It doesn't matter," Summer finally said, guilt weighing down on her like a sackcloth. "I'll go with them, but only because you asked."

"Thank you," Martha replied.

Elsie rushed inside, her eyes wide with hurt and concern, her face flushed. "Summer?"

"I'm sorry, Mama," Summer said. "I didn't mean what I said. I'll come and stay with y'all for a few days."

"Oh, honey, I'm so glad."

Mack followed Elsie, his face white with worry. "Hey, are you okay?"

Summer nodded. "I'm going to the big house." Her humor didn't make anyone laugh. "I'm going to stay with my parents."

He gave her a look that combined understanding and confusion. "Okay. Need me to take you back to the center?"

"We'll take her after we tour the house," James said, his cowboy boots announcing his entry into the room. He looked relieved to hear that Summer had changed her mind.

Summer noticed her grandfather was staying in the kitchen, away from the fray. Probably wise. And she also noticed Mack's watchful eyes on her as she reluctantly walked through the house with her parents.

"Pretty impressive," her father said, nodding his approval, his snakeskin boots clicking on the hardwood floors.

"Mack, I should have hired you when we were designing and building our house," Elsie cooed, obviously thrilled to be showing off to a newcomer. "Don't you just love a man who is handy around the house?" she asked anyone who might be inclined to agree.

"I know I sure do," Martha said, joining in the gleeful celebration.

Summer stood back, glancing from her parents to Mack. She could see his discomfort and she had to wonder if he felt uncomfortable for himself, or for her. Probably both.

Now she was glad she'd told him some of the history of her relationship, or lack thereof, with her parents. At least he understood her reservations about going to stay with her parents.

"I don't want to do this," she whispered to him as they were leaving the farm earlier.

"Really? I would have never guessed."

"Does it show that much?"

"Like you've just had a root canal. Stop frowning."

"Do you promise to come and rescue me if I shout out?"

"I promise."

The look in his eyes had told her he'd do just that. That brought Summer a comfort she wasn't accustomed to having. A nice, safe security that had given her the courage to go back to Golden Vista and toss her things in her duffel bag while her parents visited with the administrators and office staff.

Martha had hugged Summer tightly as she was leaving. "I'm so proud of you, honey. Use this time to get things sorted out with your parents. It's precious time, Summer. Use it wisely."

I'm doing this for you, Memaw, she told herself now, gritting her teeth with each step. But if she were truly honest, Summer knew she was also doing this for her own peace of mind. Part of that healing process, she supposed. She couldn't get on with her life and make those changes if she was mired in anger and regret. And besides, she had lots of questions for her parents. Lots.

While her mother busied herself pouring fresh iced tea that the maid had provided, Summer sank into a heavy cream leather chair and again thought back over the afternoon. When she'd seen her parents standing there, her whole world had shifted. It made her remember all those other times she'd seen them, the times her heart had filled with hope that maybe they'd come home for good this time.

How many times had she been disappointed? How many times had her grandmother had to hold her while she cried herself to sleep because they'd left yet again?

Her mother's grating voice brought her back to the here and now. "I invited Mama and Daddy out to dinner tonight. We'll grill steaks by the pool. Oh, and I invited Mack Riley, too."

Summer felt the rush of relief move throughout her body, only to clash with the universal assumption that paired her with Mack at every gathering lately. Somehow, in spite of her firm denial regarding a romance with Mack, knowing that he would be here did make her feel a whole lot better about things. But all of these spiraling feelings were a bit overwhelming. Things were changing again, too fast for her to absorb and accept.

"That sounds nice," she managed to reply to her mother. "We can all have a good, long visit."

"You don't have to be so sarcastic," Elsie retorted, her gold coin bracelet jingling as she clinked ice into a glass.

"I didn't think I was being sarcastic," Summer replied, all of her old insecurities hitting the surface.

"You don't feel comfortable here, do you, darlin'?"

"Should I, Mother?"

"This is your home."

"No, you and Daddy sold the only home I've ever known."

"Summer, this is getting very tiresome."

"I'm just getting started."

"So…instead of spending time with your poor old daddy and me, you intend to taunt us and tease us at every turn."

"Works for me."

"You are so stubborn."

"Guess I got that naturally."

Elsie sank down on the loveseat across from Summer, then propped her feet up on the matching leather ottoman. "If your father were here—"

"Well, he's not, is he?" Summer pointed out. "Couldn't wait to get to the golf course and brag with all his buddies."

"He'll be here for dinner."

"I won't hold my breath on that."

"You are being completely nasty."

Summer decided her mother was right. Lowering her head, she willed her expression to soften. "I'm sorry. I promised Memaw—"

Elsie's hand flew to her coiffured hair. "So you only came here because my mama made you?"

"Something like that."

Summer watched as her mother blinked back tears. Crocodile tears probably. But then when her mother burst into heaving sobs, Summer became really concerned.

"Mother?"

Elsie sniffed, threw up a hand. "I…so wanted us to be friends again, Summer. I…I need a friend right now."

Summer shot out of her chair and fell down on the ottoman, one hand touching her mother's arm. "Mommy, I've never seen you like this."

"I've never *been* like this," Elsie said, tears streaming down her face. "Honestly, I think I'm losing my mind."

Summer felt a strange shifting inside her heart, like clay crumbling into jagged pieces. "What's wrong?"

Elsie looked up at her, mascara smeared around her eyes. "It's your father. He… I think he wants a divorce."

Summer shut the door to her mother's bedroom, the scent of Chanel No. 5 wafting out into the hallway after her. Taking the tray of herbal tea down to the kitchen, Summer was careful not to make too much noise in the echoing house. The maid took the tray with a wan smile.

Which left Summer to wander around with her thoughts rolling ahead of her like tumbleweeds. Her mother had needed her. Her parents might be getting a divorce.

Not used to being the nurturer to her mother, Summer thought back on their conversation. Elsie had seemed so small and vulnerable, sitting there on the cushiony loveseat, pouring out her heart to Summer.

"I can't tell Mama and Daddy. It would just kill them."

"Why are you telling me?"

"Because I knew you'd understand," Elsie said on a weak voice. "Baby, you do this kind of stuff for a living right? I mean, you counsel people."

Summer was both astonished and amazed at her mother's words. Her mother wanted her to *counsel* them? Her own parents? How in the world was she supposed to do that, when she didn't even begin to understand them?

But Summer had sat with her mother, talking to her quietly, soothing her battered nerves until she had finally convinced Elsie to drink some chamomile tea and take a long nap. Apparently, James had been acting very strangely lately.

"He's just not himself. He's quiet and moody. I can't seem to please him. I just know he's found someone else. I mean, I've tried to do everything to please him, I've tried to stay young-looking and slim. I've helped him with what's left of his rodeo glory, but that's about all dried up. Maybe he blames me for that, but I can't help the man growing old. He thinks he's a has-been. Maybe that makes me a has-been, too."

"You're not that, Mother," Summer had said. "You're just both middle-aged now. The rodeo days are over. Maybe it's time to accept that and find something else to do with the rest of your lives."

That statement had only caused Elsie to burst into tears yet again. "I might not have a life, if your father leaves me."

"Now I need some counseling myself," Summer whispered, still in shock. Of all the sure things in her life, her parents' love for each other had always been one of the most outstanding. If that love, so unshakable, so solid, so intense, was about to cave, then she didn't hold out much hope for the rest of humanity. She looked up at the huge iron-and-stone cross hanging on the wall in the den and for the first time in a long time, she turned to God. *I really need You now, Lord.*

The doorbell rang. Summer hurried to answer it, afraid it would wake her mother. When she opened it and saw Mack standing there, her heart lurched. She had to catch her breath. It was if God had heard her plea and sent the one man who might be able to help Summer.

"Boy, am I glad to see you," she said. Then she grabbed his arm and hauled him into the house.

"Good to see you, too," Mack said, pleased that Summer seemed so all fired up to get him inside. "I brought your car for you. I'll catch a ride back to the center with your grandparents."

"Good, fine." She marched him down the long hall and into the spacious den. "Sit."

"Okay." He sat down, watching as she paced before the fireplace. Then he noticed the hollow look in her eyes, the frown on her face. And he saw that her hands were shaking. "You really *don't* like being here, do you?"

"It's weird. Especially right now," she said on a low whisper. "Things are…complicated."

Not liking the way her eyes darted toward the stairs, he said, "Want to clue me in?"

"There's something not right here, Mack."

"Yeah, well, that's obvious. But you promised your grandmother."

"Not that," she said, her hands on her hips. "I'm trying, Mack. Really I am. And I think it's probably a good thing I decided to stay here for a while."

Mack was getting dizzy, watching her whirl around, so when she passed close, he grabbed her arm and pulled her onto the couch with him. "What's going on, Summer?"

She sank down beside him. "I shouldn't be doing this. I shouldn't be so happy to see you. But right before you rang the doorbell, I…I asked God to help me."

Mack let out a whistle. "Must be serious, since you said you'd quit talking to God."

"It is serious."

He saw that seriousness in her eyes. He was so close, he could see the flecks of deep blue in her irises. "So, what did God tell you?"

"Nothing yet. But then you showed up."

"I always have had good timing."

"Don't make fun," she said, her eyes bright with a fear that scared him.

"Then talk to me. Tell me what's the matter."

"You can't tell anyone."

"Okay."

She let out a sigh, pushed at her hair, looked away. "My parents might be getting a divorce."

Mack had to shake his head. "What?"

"That's exactly what I said when my mother poured her heart out to me. Not less than an hour ago, we had probably the longest conversation we've ever had in our lives, with her doing most of the talking and me doing most of the listening. Mack, she…she needed me."

Not sure how to respond, he said, "Well,

I guess that's a good thing. Even though it's a bad situation."

But Summer shook her head, ran a hand over the grainy leather of the couch. "But why now, when her life is in a major crisis? I don't mind helping my mother, but I just wish she'd needed me…during all the happy times, too." She put a hand to her mouth. "I don't know if I can do this. I don't know if I can be strong enough to help her through this. What am I doing to do?"

Mack saw the panic on her face, felt it in the way she seemed to be slowly shaking. "Hey, now," he said as he reached for her, "it's gonna be all right. Maybe they just had a fight or something."

"I think it's more than a fight," she said, falling into his arms. "I think it's something that's been brewing for a very long time. And I never even knew, because I didn't take the time to find out how they were doing. I didn't want to know the details of their life, because I was so jealous of that life."

Mack pulled her close, unable to stop himself. Summer was one of the toughest people he knew, but right now she seemed very fragile. "It's gonna work out, I promise. You have to hang tough and help your mother. Maybe it's payback time."

"What does that mean?" she asked, her whisper vibrating against his chest.

Mack closed his eyes, let the scent of her citrus shampoo wash over him. "It means maybe your mother will see that she has a daughter who loves her and wants to be close to her, and now, you have that chance."

Summer lifted her head, her eyes going wide. "That's what Memaw told me. That this was my chance."

Mack smiled down at her. "Then I'd say God heard your prayers, Summer. And he's giving you a chance to bridge that gap you've always felt between your parents and you."

"What if I can't cross that bridge, mend that gap?"

"I think you can," Mack replied. "I know you can. You try so hard to hide it, but I think there is a lot of love inside you. And a lot of faith."

Summer gave him a grudging smile. "I really didn't want to like you."

"I know," Mack said. Then he lowered his head and kissed her, taking in the sweet, slow way she responded. Summer seemed to melt into his kiss, a reluctant sigh escaping as she kissed him back. He could almost read her mind as she finally gave in and let him hold her close. Hesitant. Scared. Longing. And then, accepting and needing to be touched and held. He felt all the same things and marveled at how much trusting someone was akin to accepting faith in God.

Summer pulled back, her eyes wide with a mixture of triumph and trepidation. "And I really didn't want to kiss you."

"I know," he said. "Which is why you're going to do it again, right?"

"Uh-huh," she said as she tugged him close again.

Mack enjoyed the kiss and let it settle around him. Then he opened his eyes, held his head back for a smile—

And saw James Maxwell's scowling reflection in the big mirror over the fireplace, staring him down.

Chapter Twelve

"Mr. Maxwell!"

Mack jumped up, away from the warmth of Summer's embrace. Summer followed, surprised to find her father staring at them with thunder in his eyes. But right now, she was so angry about her mother's revelations and confused by Mack's sweet kiss, she didn't care what her father thought.

"Well, well," James said, the stern expression on his face making him look as dangerous as the bulls he used to ride. "I leave for a couple of hours and what do I come home to? Summer—with a boy. Some things never change, I reckon." He gave Mack a broad grin. "I can't tell you how many times I came home to catch her with some football player or race-car driver. Even threw in a couple of rodeo rookies, I think just to get to me. My daughter has always been good at attracting the boys."

"He's not exactly a boy, Daddy," Summer pointed out. "And you only came home on rare occasions, so how do you know who all I dated?"

James drew back, frowning. "I can see your attitude hasn't changed much either."

Summer got up, rubbing her hands down her shorts. "This is different, Daddy. Mack's a grown man, and…he's a friend. A good friend. And in case you haven't noticed, I'm all grown up, too."

"Oh, I noticed that right off the bat," James said, a soft smile splitting his frown. Then he turned to Mack, a kind of regret and longing moving over his weathered face. "She always did break hearts. Be careful, son. Be very careful."

Summer watched Mack relax, but she was grateful for his hand reaching for hers. "I think I can handle things, sir."

"I sure hope so. She's a lot like her mama. Stubborn and unreasonable and determined to do things her way. Speaking of your mama, where is she?"

"She's upstairs resting," Summer said, careful that she didn't lash out at her father until she'd had a chance to hear his side of the story. "I'm worried about her. She was so tired."

James looked worried, too. "Elsie, resting in the middle of the day? That don't sound right. Your mama usually goes full-throttle until the wee hours. Can't hold her back. Not one little bit, even when I try."

Summer shot a glance toward Mack. He gave her a warning look. Trying to stay neutral for now, Summer said, "Well, you did have a long flight home, and Mama and I had a good talk. She just needed to take a nap."

"Hope she'll be down for dinner," James said, satisfied for now. "It'll be so nice to have the whole family gathered together."

Summer saw the sincerity in her father's eyes and wondered when her parents had gotten so old and mellow. Her father was still a handsome man, tall and sinewy. But he looked tired and there was a darkness around his eyes. His almost-black hair was shot through with shimmers of gray. And he did seem genuinely concerned about her mother.

Summer stared up at him, seeing so much there in the lines and angles of her father's face. And she realized that she, too, had missed out on a lot of things. Simply because she was so stubborn and so stuck in dwelling on the past. She'd certainly had plenty of opportunities through the years to visit her parents, both here in Athens, and around the world. It wasn't as if she didn't have the means to buy a plane ticket now and then. But her pride and pain had always held her back.

Maybe God had brought them all home for a reason.

She looked over at Mack again. "Mack, would you mind if I have a few minutes to visit with my Daddy?"

Mack lifted his brows, then turned to James. "I don't mind a bit. I'll just go outside and check out that nice swimming pool."

"There's extra swimsuits in the cabana, if you want to take a dip," Summer said, hoping Mack would understand.

He seemed to. "I just might do that. It's been a hot day today. Y'all don't worry about me. Take your time catching up." The look he gave Summer indicated that she needed to do just that.

James watched Mack head toward the back of the house. "Nice fellow."

"Yes, he is," Summer said, remembering the way Mack's kiss had sent her reeling. "But Daddy, don't read anything into this. Mack and I are just—"

James held up a hand. "I know—really good friends." His smile was bittersweet. "You know, I've always hoped you'd find a good man and settle down. I worry about you, suga'."

Summer came around the couch, watching as her father poured himself a glass of mineral water. "Did you worry about me when you were on the rodeo circuit, Daddy?"

James gave her a resigned look. "You know I did."

"Actually, I could never be sure," Summer replied, her bitterness turning to an aching wound that needed to heal. Suddenly, she felt tired. Tired of holding on to this grudge, tired of blaming her parents for everything. Maybe her grandmother was right. It was time to take a chance and find her way back to the fold. "Daddy, can we talk? I mean, really talk?"

James grinned. "I thought that was what we were doing."

Summer motioned to the chairs. "Let's sit down."

"Don't mind if I do," James said. He tossed his black cowboy hat on a nearby table. "Got mighty hot out on that golf course."

For the first time, Summer noticed the way he held his body, as if it hurt to stand up straight. "Are you okay, Daddy?"

"This old back," James said, wincing as he settled into the soft leather. "I guess I shouldn't have played such a vigorous game today. But you know me. I like the competition. Sure don't like losing, though."

Summer waited for him to get settled, wondering if she should ask him about what her mother had told her. According to Elsie, James had become withdrawn and subdued lately. They hadn't enjoyed their travels to Mexico this time, as they had in the past. Elsie implied that James no longer confided in her, that he seemed uninterested in her. She was sure he was either seeing another woman, or on the verge of just flat-out leaving her.

"Why did y'all come home?" Summer asked her father, hoping he might open up to her.

James smiled at her, his eyes as bright and blue as her own. "We wanted to see you, of course. Your mama read your e-mail telling us you were coming home, and right away, she started fretting. And she was worried about Martha and Jesse. You know, selling the house was hard on all of us."

"Was it really?" Summer asked, holding back on the condemnation she'd felt since coming home.

"Yes, honey. We wrestled back and forth with this decision. But I want you to know, we didn't go into this lightly. Your mother and I let Jesse and Martha make the final decision. You have to know, Summer, that they will always be taken care of. Always."

"Why couldn't they just stay at the farm?"

James leaned forward, winced again, his hand shooting to his back. "Well, we all wanted that, even talked about hiring them a companion. But they didn't want a stranger hovering around them all the time. You see, one day about a year ago, your grandmother found your papaw passed out near the pond. He'd had a dizzy spell. Luckily, he just got a bit overheated and he was fine. But that scared Martha and it really scared your mama. That's when we asked them about considering moving to Golden Vista."

Summer imagined her grandfather, all alone and unconscious, and felt a tinge of remorse over her recent outbursts. "I guess I thought they'd be around forever."

James nodded. "I wish we could all be

around forever, but time marches on, suga'." The darkness around his eyes seemed to widen with that statement, but his wry smile was intact. "The thing about Golden Vista is I'd invested in the place myself—sold the investment group the land the place is built on, helped design the entire complex. So I knew it in and out, top to bottom. I knew they'd be taken care of there."

Summer sat silently for a while, then said, "Okay, I can live with that. It's taken some getting used to, but I can certainly see that the retirement center is safe and comfortable. They seem to be happy."

"They are," James assured her. "And that's what matters."

"What about you and Mama?" she asked, holding her breath for the answer. She'd never actually considered that her parents might not be happy together. They had always seemed so caught up in each other, Summer couldn't imagine them any other way.

James's face went blank. "What do you mean?"

"I mean, are y'all still happy, traveling around like nomads? Don't you ever just want to find a place to settle down?"

James looked surprised, then sheepish. "It's hard to say, honey. There are a lot of things I want, but wanting don't make it happen. You know, there never was very much money to be made in the rodeo. It was all about being the center of attention, about being a star. I've been blessed with a grand fortune, thanks to the Maxwell holdings. I milked that and my rodeo days for all they were worth. I guess the gravy train is finally drying up."

Shocked, Summer asked, "Are you saying you've lost money? That you and mother are in financial trouble?"

"Of course not," James said, scoffing at the very idea. "Your Uncle Richard has always taken care of our finances and he'd never let that happen, no matter how much we've tried to spend all our dough. I mean, the rodeo circuit isn't what it used to be. I guess I'm trying to tell you that your ol' daddy is a has-been. Washed out and washed up."

"But you had a good career. You should be proud of that. You've got friends all over the place. And you've had a good life, haven't you?"

James nodded. "I have. Being the middle child, I had to find my own way of getting attention. And I did that in my rodeo heyday. But now, well, I'm struggling. I'm asking myself, was my whole life a big waste?"

Summer stared over at her father, wondering about the paradox that made up her parents. They were a constant source of wonder to her, two people whom she loved and resented at the same time. But right now, to her surprise, the love was fast overtaking the resentment. They were home, and that counted in Summer's book now more than it ever had before. That, and her father's admissions.

"Daddy, are you having a crisis of some sort?"

James laughed. "No, I don't think so. I'm just getting old and…well, losing Stuart made me stop and think about my own mortality." He looked over at her, his eyes bright with regret and hope. "I don't want to waste any more time, honey. I'm tired. I want to find some new kind of meaning in my life."

"There's nothing wrong with that," Summer said, beginning to see what was really happening in her parents' marriage. She reached over and touched her father's leathery hand. "I believe you and Mama still have a lot to give, Daddy. I think you can find your way through this if you look for the opportunities ahead."

"And that would be membership in AARP, right?" James said, his tone teasing.

"Well, that does have its perks," Summer replied. "But you could serve on any number of philanthropic boards. You could find some sort of part-time work, maybe helping troubled teens learn about horses and the rodeo."

James looked thoughtful for a minute. "In other words, instead of wallowing in self-pity, find myself something to keep me busy, right?"

"Exactly," Summer said, smiling over at him.

"But what about your mama?" James asked, sounding frightened.

"What about her?"

He leaned forward, lowered his voice. "What if she—what if she's disappointed in me. You know how she loves to travel and entertain."

"She can still do both," Summer replied, amazed that both her parents were having a major self-esteem problem right now. After all those years of marriage and togetherness, they still weren't completely sure about each other. That only reinforced Summer's own misgivings in the love department.

"You should talk to her," Summer said. "Tell Mama how you're feeling. Tell her what you want to do with the rest of your life."

James nodded. "I sure hope I'm just as smart as you when I finally do grow up."

Touched, Summer said, "Maybe we're all growing up, at last."

James struggled to get out of his chair.

"Maybe. And maybe the best place to do that is right here at home, huh?"

Summer felt tears pricking at her eyes. "I think so, Daddy."

James pulled her close, hugging her to him. "I didn't hug you enough when you were little. I intend to work on that some while we're here, honey."

Summer didn't cry. Instead, she felt a surge of joy as her father's strong arms held her close.

Maybe this time, she'd be the one to leave first. And maybe this time, she could leave knowing that her parents still loved each other *and her.*

Mack stood looking down into the blue waters of the pool, his mind still on kissing Summer. His mind on how that kiss had affected him. He'd taken a dip, all right. Just to cool the mixed emotions and sweet longings he felt inside his soul. The water was great, but Mack was still drowning in that kiss. His cell phone rang, causing him to throw down his towel and fumble for it. "Hello?"

"Mack, it's Belinda."

Silence. She'd finally tracked him down. "How did you get this number?"

"That doesn't matter. Don't hang up on me, please."

Mack closed his eyes, held a breath, said a prayer. "What do you want?"

He heard her intake of breath, heard the quiver of her words. "I want to see you. It's really important."

"Belinda, we don't need to rehash things. It's over this time. It's been over for a very long time."

"I know that," she said. He thought he heard a sob, but then Belinda was so good at acting, it couldn't have been a real one. "I know things can never be the same between us, but I really need to see you."

"I don't think—"

"I can't talk about this over the phone," she said, her tone turning to a plea. "I'm sorry to bother you, but I had to find you. I only need a few minutes, to explain."

"Explain what?" Mack asked, confused. His heart was hammering a warning beat, but he couldn't help but feel that old tug again. "Just tell me, Belinda."

"I can't. Not like this. This is too important. I have to see you for so many reasons, and if you won't come here, then I'll just have to come there."

"No." He didn't want her here in Athens. He'd made a good life here and he wouldn't go back into that crazy, Tilt-A-Whirl of a life they'd had together. "Don't come here. And I can't come there, wherever *there* is for you right now. So if you've got something to say, say it now."

"I...I can't do that, not like this," she said. "I'll be in touch."

Mack heard a beep and then silence. "Belinda?" She'd hung up. He sank down on a patio chair, wondering what Belinda would do next. What if she just showed up in Athens? What then? Grabbing his shirt, Mack jerked it on.

"Bad news?"

He pivoted at Summer's question. "What?"

"The way you're staring at your phone, you must have gotten bad news? A leaky pipe in one of the apartments? A gopher tearing up your cabbage roses?"

Mack managed a shaky laugh. "I wish." Then he shrugged. "Just someone I knew once, wanting to get together and share old times."

She lifted her chin. "About old times—just how many hearts have *you* broken, Mack Riley?"

"None, that I can recall," he said, the guilt of his relationship with Belinda weighing on him. But he couldn't bring himself to talk about that again with Summer. "You know how that goes."

"Yeah, I sure do," she said, shaking her head. "I guess we don't need to go into detail right now."

Mack managed to shake off the bad feeling Belinda's call had provoked. "No, not just yet." Then he looked into Summer's eyes. "But one day, I do need to tell you everything." He shrugged. "You know most of what went on with Belinda, but you need to hear the whole story."

He saw the doubt clouding her blue eyes. "Was that her on the phone?"

He gave her a silent nod.

"She wants to see you again?"

"Yes." Seeing the doubt in Summer's eyes, he added, "But I don't want to see her. I told her to leave me alone."

"She must have really messed with your head."

"She did." He got up, pushed a hand through his wet hair. "Can we change the subject, please?"

Summer gave him a knowing look. "So you do have secrets, just like the rest of us."

"A few," he said, hoping she'd leave it at that for now. "Some things are hard to reveal."

He watched as her eyes changed from a cloudy blue to crystal-clear and full of resolve. "I've got a few things I don't want to talk about either. But…we'll save that for another day. I'm not ready to get into anything heavy. I've got enough to figure out with what's brewing between my parents." She sank down on a chaise. "But I did have a good talk with my daddy, at least."

Mack walked over to her, took her hand in his. "You're very brave, taking on a tough situation like this."

"I'm a highly trained professional," she whispered, her voice full of sarcasm, her smile mocking.

"You are a pro, but…this is your parents."

"How do I try to understand and counsel two people I don't even really know?"

Mack didn't know how to answer that. "I guess you start with love. You do love your parents, right?"

She nodded. "I never realized how much until today. They've grown older, Mack. They…I think they might have come home for good this time." She pushed at her bangs. "But what if they came home, only to go their separate ways? I might not ever get to see them in the role I've always longed for. I wanted a set of traditional parents, not some jet-set party animals. Maybe they just partied themselves out, until there was nothing left."

Mack sat down beside her and pulled her close. "I think there's plenty left. You might not be the one to bring them back together, but you could be the one to bring them home for good."

And yourself, too, Mack thought. But he didn't voice that to Summer. He couldn't voice that silent wish he had inside his racing heart, because he wasn't so sure he should even be wishing it. Not after he'd just talked to Belinda and had all those old feelings pulling at him to remind him of his shortcomings.

But it sure would be nice if Summer would stay home this time, too. Here with him.

Summer looked up at him, her eyes telling him that she could almost read his thoughts. "A homecoming," she said with a sigh. "I've always dreamed of that. But not like this. Mack, I have to try and help my parents."

"That's the spirit," he said, proud of her for turning this around. "Whatever is happening with them, I have a feeling they need their daughter right now."

She blinked, her eyes misty. "I've... never felt needed before. Not by my parents. In my work in New York, yes, which is why I poured myself into it, to the point of losing myself completely. But that was so different from this. There I had to be objective and I had to hold everything inside. I don't know if I can do that with my folks."

"You love them. Show them that love, Summer."

"Do you think my love can save whatever is wrong with them?"

"I can't answer that. But it doesn't hurt to try."

Summer shook her head, turned to stare at the shimmering pool. "Funny, I always resented my parents being so in love. Now, I'm praying that they still are."

Mack pulled at her long hair. "I'm praying right along with you."

Summer leaned back into his embrace, smiling as he settled his nose against the top of her head. "I haven't prayed in a very long time."

Mack kissed her hair. "But even when you weren't praying, God was listening."

"Well, I hope He's still listening. I can't

bear to see my parents torn apart and hurt. I won't let that happen."

Mack closed his eyes, wished for Summer to find peace and guidance from above. And he also asked God to help him find that same peace. Because he had a feeling that Belinda Lewis wasn't through with him yet. And maybe, neither was God.

Chapter Thirteen

July hit Athens like a steamy blanket being tossed over a drooping clothesline. The whole countryside was limp with lack of rain, parched and damp at the same time. The humidity only made everything look worse. Mack was constantly having to water the grass and the flowers at Golden Vista. How he managed to keep them alive in this heat was beyond Summer.

But then, everything about Mack Riley seemed to intrigue her these days, Summer thought as she made herself a tall glass of water with lemon. The man was good at his job and good with handling the myriad problems that came with dealing with senior citizens. Lost animals, misplaced medicine, loneliness, sickness and ailments, confusion, doctor's appointments and field trips that went from bad to worse—these were some of the things Mack and the rest of the staff at Golden Vista handled on a daily basis. Sometimes death hung over the place like the humidity, and sometimes a resident would not come home after a rushed hospital visit or a frantic call for the emergency ambulance. But in spite of losing yet another old person, Mack always had a ready smile and kind words to help console the family. His patience and understanding surpassed any dedication Summer had ever witnessed before. And he managed to include her in everything, forcing her to stay involved and just one step ahead of her own depression and misgivings.

And the ladies who managed Golden Vista thought Mack had hung the moon.

"He's a pretty thing, isn't he?" Cissie, the office manager, had cooed earlier today while Summer sat in the office with them, going over the details of the festival.

"Easy on the eye, for sure," Pamela, the events coordinator, had replied.

"A dream to work with," their boss Lola had agreed. "We're so lucky to have Mack here."

Then the three ladies had all turned to Summer, their eager expressions and smug smiles just begging for details.

"Are y'all an item?" Cissie asked, her Southern drawl stretched with innocence. "That's what we keep hearing, you know."

"Can't you tell?" Pamela answered, her blond hair falling against her cheeks. "The way that man looks at her—I'd say he's got a bad crush on this one."

"I think you two should get back to the business at hand, which is helping Summer finish up these plans for our festival," Lola said, her glasses perched on her nose. Then she glanced over at Summer, a dreamy smile plastered on her face. "If I was twenty years younger, girl, I'd sure give you a run for your money with that one."

"It's not like that," Summer insisted. "Mack and I are just good friends."

"Yeah, right," Cissie retorted. "That's what Miss Gladys tells us about her and Mr. Maroney, too. But they've taken to sharing just about every meal together. And they sit together on the bus. Yeah, they're *real* good friends."

"I think I saw them holding hands the other day," Pamela added.

"Well, that's sweet," Summer replied, "but you won't catch Mack and I doing that, I promise."

"At least not while anyone's looking, right?" Cissie asked, grinning.

Summer grinned now as she remembered the gentle ribbing. It was hard to have a romantic relationship in such a tight-knit community. Who knew there were so many romantics and matchmakers living at Golden Vista?

While Summer had been up to her eyeballs in planning the big Fourth of July festival, she'd also grown very close to most of the lovable residents of the retirement complex. It would be hard to leave all the seniors who talked to her and asked her advice on everything from bursitis to baby showers. Her grandmother had pronounced Summer the unofficial counselor of Golden Vista, reminding Summer that "old people need therapy, too, honey."

Some in the worst kind of way, Summer had discovered. She'd also discovered that sitting and listening to the residents brought her a certain measure of comfort. She was contributing, so she didn't feel useless. That was something she couldn't stand, being idle and listless. She'd actually helped some of them with sickness, mending relationships with estranged family members, or dealing with the loss of a favorite pet.

This morning, Summer sat at the desk in her father's huge, paneled den, and began an e-mail to her cousins, eager to tell them about her life here.

Things here have settled into a kind of routine for me. I get up each day, check on any e-mails from the Y in New York and respond to those first. Then Mama and I do our laps in the pool. Funny, but we've had some of our best conversa-

tions after our swims, when we sit down
to have breakfast out on the back patio.
This is before the heat takes over and
we're forced inside. Then I either go to
visit Memaw and Papaw and all the other
residents at Golden Vista and help out
there, or I get together with Mack to finish the plans for the big Fourth of July Village Festival. That's all the talk at Golden
Vista.

Word has it that Mr. Maroney is going
to ask Mrs. Hanes to marry him that night,
just when the fireworks go off. Isn't that
so romantic? Those two are so cute, trying so hard to ignore each other. But
Mack keeps supplying Mr. Maroney with
flowers at every turn, and Mr. Maroney
gives them to Mrs. Hanes with such a
flourish that the whole village has noticed. He ambushes her when she's on
her way back from the beauty parlor, and
sometimes he puts the flowers on her table at dinner. She finally invited him to sit
with her the other night. Now they share
all their meals together.

Oh, and Mack has given me flowers,
too. Wildflowers and daisies, sunflowers

that are just bursting with bright yellow blossoms. He's not like other men. Not very traditional—he thinks roses are only pretty when they're fresh-picked with dew on them. Refuses to order them from a florist. But flowers do not mean a thing. We are good friends now, at least. I don't resent him anymore for buying the farm. How could I, when he's got the house in mint condition and now he's working on the yards and fields. The farm looks better than ever.

I'm progressing with Mama and Daddy, too. Although they seem okay, I still can't get to the bottom of why my mother thinks my father wants a divorce. I think Daddy's just going through some sort of change-of-life crisis, and he won't talk to her about it. So she assumes the worst. You know Mama. She flutters around like a ladybug, decorating the over-decorated house, shopping for things she doesn't need, having her nails done, her hair done. She tells me about her day or invites me to join her. But she won't go into detail about things with Daddy too much. They both seem sad at times, but I can't get either of them just to talk to each other. They both confide in me, which is really surprising, but there is so much more to learn about them. So I guess I'll keep trying. Who knew that I'd come home to so much: my grandparents living in a retirement village, my parents home and somehow different. And Mack as my new best friend. I miss New York and my work, but I have to admit being here has helped me to slow down and regain my strength. And helping the old folks has shown me that we all just want to be loved and needed.

April, I should be in peak condition for your wedding. I can't wait until we all get together to try on our gowns and have that shower we promised you. And Autumn, you'd better make it home for that! And the wedding.

Oh, Autumn, did you ever find out what's cooking with your daddy? Is he still acting strange? What is it with our parents these days, anyway? Love to both of you, Summer.

Summer sent the e-mail then signed off the computer. She had lots to do today. She had to check with the vendors for the festival and talk to the kitchen staff at Golden Vista about the food booths. Then she had to meet with Mack to go over the layout of the booths and how they'd handle parking.

"Honey, are you still here?"

"In the office, Mama," Summer called, still mystified that she was actually living with her parents and getting along with them.

"Oh, good," Elsie said, her silk teal-colored caftan flowing out around her like butterfly wings. "I was hoping I'd catch you before you got busy."

"What is it?" Summer asked, on eggshells these days hoping her mother would have good news instead of bad regarding her parents' marriage.

"Nothing," Elsie said, smiling. "Just that…well, I wanted to thank you, honey, for listening to all my tales of woe about your father."

"Mama, I don't mind," Summer told her. While she worried about her father's odd behavior and her mother's fears, she had at least grown closer to both her parents. "Where is Daddy?" she asked. Her father was usually gone most mornings by the time she got up, even though she still woke up early just as she had in New York.

"He had a meeting with his lawyers or something," Elsie said. "I have no idea what he's up to."

Summer saw the worry cresting in her mother's eyes, and wished her father would just be honest with Elsie. Elsie had on very little makeup this morning. Summer saw the freckles and age spots dotting her mother's skin, but to her, Elsie had never looked more beautiful. "You don't think—"

Elsie fidgeted with removing the dead fronds from the parlor fern in the corner. "Hard to say. We have been talking more lately. I did what you suggested and tried to question your father tactfully about his comings and goings. He didn't exactly tell me anything, just kissed me and told me not to worry so much. But he turned before he left this morning and told me he loves me." She sighed. "He seemed like the James Maxwell I've always loved.

Amazing, how one crumb of hope can make a soul soar."

Summer sat looking up at her mother. Elsie stood by the arched windows overlooking the backyard, her reddish-blond hair shining like a halo in the morning sun. "Mama, you are still so beautiful. Daddy has to see that."

Elsie brushed at tears. "I hope he does. Do you think he sees me as old and washed up?"

Summer got up to come and take her mother's arms, thinking her father had pretty much asked her the same thing about himself. "That's silly. You've worked hard to stay in shape and you—"

"I know. I've visited every plastic surgeon known to man, in several countries. But I never had any work done. Maybe I should check myself into one of those private clinics and have the whole nine yards done, from head to toe."

"Mama, changing yourself outside can't fix the pain inside," Summer said. "I've seen some of the richest women in New York, broke and broken, simply because they didn't have enough gumption to leave abusive situations. They didn't want to give up their salons and shopping sprees, their Botox injections and their chauffeurs and mansions. They would rather put social standing before their own health and self-esteem." She turned in her chair. "Mama, you don't need any of that. I can't speak for Daddy, but I really think he's going through a lot right now. He's still mourning Uncle Stuart's death, and I think he's realizing that he can't be young and carefree forever. You should talk to him and just be honest with him. He needs you, Mama."

Elsie lifted a hand to Summer's hair. "You are an amazing woman, do you know that?"

Summer never imagined she'd be so touched by words coming from her mother, but she was. "I'm not that amazing. I just have a job to do."

"And you do it. You did everything to make me proud. You struck out on your own and made a life for yourself, in spite of your mother's shortcomings."

Summer wasn't ready to get down to

the nitty-gritty of the past, even though she knew it would help both of them. That confrontation she'd always imagined now seemed petty and mean-spirited. And her mother seemed so frail and small. Fragile. "I'm the one with shortcomings, Mama, trust me."

"Oh, I don't believe that," Elsie said, her smile bittersweet and strained. "I left you so many times. Left you behind, knowing it was so wrong."

Summer's heart hurt with the pain of that confession. "Why did you do it?"

Elsie shook her head. "It's hard to explain, hard to understand. I was so afraid I'd lose your father if I let him get out there away from me. I smothered him with love, and I forced him always to take me with him." She lowered her head. "I should have been smothering you with love, darlin'. I should have put my foot down and told your father that we needed to put you first. I'm so sorry I didn't see that. And the real kicker is I might lose both of you because of it."

Summer's legs seemed to turn to jelly.

She sank down on a chair, her eyes locked on her mother's face. "I never thought—"

"You never thought you'd hear me say that?" Elsie asked, sniffing. "Well, this situation with your daddy and me has got me to thinking about a lot of things. I always knew you were safe here with Mama and Daddy, so I pushed any guilt or worries aside, telling myself next time, I'd stay here with you, next time I'd convince your father to settle down. Then next time would roll around and there I'd go, off to yet another adventure. I think it's all finally catching up with me."

"Better late than never, right?" Summer said, her heart sinking with the sure knowledge that her mother was only turning to her because Elsie was so afraid of losing her father. "Is that it, Mother? You think if Daddy leaves you, you'll be all alone? So you're trying to mend fences with me, just so someone will be there with you in your old age?"

Elsie looked shocked, a slight flush rising over her freckles. "Is that how you see me, Summer? You think I'd just use my own daughter that way?"

Summer shrugged, starting to gather her paperwork. "Honestly, I wonder, I mean, here we are making polite conversation, when we both know there is still a huge gap between us."

"I thought we were trying to mend that gap," Elsie replied, hurt causing her to frown. "I thought that you cared—"

"I do care, Mama," Summer said, wishing she'd learn to choose her words more carefully. "But what happens if this rift between you and Daddy suddenly ends? What then? Will you leave with him? Will I be the one left alone again?"

Elsie sank down on a chair, then pushed a hand through her tousled hair. The guilt on her face told Summer what she needed to know.

Summer started for the door, but Elsie grabbed her by the arm. "Summer, I'm trying. I don't know what's going on with your father, but I've never had any reason to doubt his love until now." Her eyes glistened as her voice became a whisper. "I've never been very good at being alone, darlin'."

Summer pulled her arm away. "Well,

maybe you should learn to deal with it, Mama, the way I had to learn to deal with it."

Elsie put a hand to her mouth. "Is that how you felt? All alone? But, honey, you had Memaw and Papaw."

"Yes," Summer said, whirling around. "I had my grandparents and I loved them dearly, but I always had to wonder why my own parents couldn't love me the way my grandparents did. No one has ever been able to explain that to me, Mama." She grabbed her car keys. "You know, for the first time in my life, I thought you might actually need me. I thought we were getting somewhere. But now I can see that I'm only a substitute for Daddy. I don't want to be a substitute. I want to be first in someone's heart, just once. You just don't get that, do you, Mama?"

Elsie looked up at her, her face white with shock and hurt. "Summer, you've got it all wrong, honey. I love you. Your father adores you. We're here now, aren't we?"

Summer nodded. "For now, yes. But only until something better comes along. Once you both figure out that old age isn't the end of the world, you'll find something to take you away. Then you'll both be out there and gone again. I can't take that this time, Mama. I just can't."

She left, shutting the front door with a soft thud that echoed the thudding inside her heart. Disappointment and resentment coursed through her with a sharp-edged precision, making her insides feel like shredded ribbons. Why had she let them get her hopes up? Why had she even bothered?

Mack could see the mad all over Summer's face as she entered the rec room at Golden Vista. She had that frown that caused her wide lips to jut out and she had that burning look in her blue, flame-tipped eyes. He watched as she headed straight to the coffeepot and poured a generous cupful into her favorite bluebonnet-etched mug.

Mack thought back over the last few days. Summer and her parents had reached a truce of sorts, or at least that's what it had looked like. She hadn't complained much lately about their glittery house or their shallow ways. She'd smiled and told him about her long talks with her mother. She'd delved into the plans for the festival with the same dedication and zeal he imagined she'd poured into her work back in New York. And she'd sat with the residents, getting to know them by name, and offering them kind but sure advice and words of comfort. Everything had been going so smoothly.

And he'd been moving right along, his feelings for Summer growing with the same steady rise as the wisteria vine that moved up the gazebo out in the courtyard of the center. Now he had to wonder what had happened to put that anger back in her eyes.

"Summer?" he called as he strolled across the tiled floor.

She turned slightly, barely acknowledging his presence. "What?"

"Good morning to you, too," he said, treading carefully.

"Hi," she said before taking a long sip of her cream-laced coffee. Then she plopped down at the table where they'd been working on the festival details, her eyes glued to the inch-thick folder of notes and printout in front of her.

"Want to talk about it?"

"No."

"Did you get up on the wrong side of the bed?"

"No, just in the wrong house."

Mack sat down beside her. "Fight with your mother?"

"No."

Mack let out a sigh. This frustrating woman could become brooding and tight-lipped as fast as a rogue thundershower could slip up on the Texas horizon. "Are you in pain?"

"Yes."

"Do you want—"

"I want to be left alone," she said, never once looking at him.

But Mack wasn't about to let her alone. No, sir. He knew her well enough after all these weeks to tell that when she said one thing, she usually really meant another. "I can't leave you alone right now. We've got a meeting with Mr. Tatum about the tents. He needs to know where to set up."

She waved a hand, still staring at the papers on the table. "Tell him to put them wherever he wants."

"Okay. But we need to decide about the children's games. Do you have enough volunteers for each booth?"

"Plenty of volunteers."

Mack sat drumming his fingers on the table, then decided to take a direct approach. "Summer, what's got this bee in your bonnet?"

She turned to him then, her big eyes going wide. "Is there something wrong with you, Mack? What part of go away do you not understand?"

Mack felt his own anger rising, but he managed to push it aside. For now. "I don't think I'm going anywhere. Not until you tell me what's wrong."

"You *can* go," she said, getting up to put her mug in the sink on the long counter. "Everybody else does."

Mack let that stew for a minute or two. "Are your parents…are they leaving again? Is that what this is all about?"

She shook her head, her shoulders slumping as she leaned into the counter. "Not yet. But they will. They always do. I should have remembered that."

Mack couldn't relate to what she was saying. His parents had rarely left him overnight when he was growing up. But he could relate to being abandoned. He thought of Belinda and wondered where she was right now. She had certainly abandoned him, rejected him, hurt him, so many times he'd lost count. If he let her back into his life, would he only be disappointed again?

"I think I know how you feel," he said finally. "You kind of let your guard down, didn't you? You let your parents back into your heart and now—"

"And now, once things are all better between my mother and father, they will be gone all over again." She turned to face Mack at last. "Why does that hurt so much, Mack?"

Mack pulled her into his arms, wishing he had the answer to that question. "Are you sure about this? I mean, are they about to up and leave Athens or something?"

She shook her head, her face muffled by the cotton of his shirt, her warmth causing him to want to kiss her again. "I just realized it this morning when I was talking to my mother. She's only turning to me because right now, she's the one being rejected, by my father. When things get right with them, I'll be out of the picture again."

Mack could understand her anger and hurt. "That would be tough, but think of how close you've become with your mother. Surely that has to count for something."

She lifted her face, her eyes misty, her determination solid. "Yes, it means I was just a convenient crutch, someone to be used and discarded."

"I don't think your mother thinks of you that way. She seems to really want to make things better between you two. And you did tell me that James and you have become close lately. Can't you trust in that and let things play out?"

Summer let out what almost passed for a sob, except that her eyes were dry. "I'm so tired of being the one who has to give out all the answers, Mack. I'm so tired of being the counselor. Who can I turn to when I have questions or complaints? Who?"

Mack held a hand to her chin. "Me," he said. Then he pointed up. "Me…and God."

Summer shook her head, pulled away. "And what if you and God both decide you can't handle me either? What if you decide there's something better, some other place you need to be, someone else who needs you more? What if both you and God abandon me, too?"

"I would never do that," Mack said, suddenly realizing he meant it with all his heart. "And God never abandons us, Summer. We might turn from Him, but He's always there, waiting for us to come home."

"I wish I could trust that," she said. "I wish I could hold on to that."

"Hold on to me," Mack said. Then he pulled her into his arms and gave her that kiss that he'd been thinking of, regardless of the prying eyes and amazed looks they'd been getting. He had to convince her that he would never abandon her or leave her or let her down.

Somehow, he had to prove that, both to Summer and to himself.

Chapter Fourteen

"Everything's ready," Summer said two days later. She turned to her grandmother. "I hope you have a good time today, Memaw."

Martha danced around, the excitement in her eyes telling Summer that this had been worth all the extra hours. "I plan to, darling. I am the most blessed woman in all of Texas. I have you and your parents here to celebrate the Fourth of July holiday with me and your grandpa, and I have you and Mack to thank for working so hard on making this festival happen. It just doesn't get any better than that."

Summer looked up to see Mack walking across the yard of Golden Vista. "You can say that again," she mumbled, drinking in the sight of him. He was dressed in his usual jeans and T-shirt, but today his shirt sported an American flag across the front. He looked content and clean-cut, the kind of man she'd seen in fashion ads in New York. Those men had only reminded her that sometimes life was fantasy. Not real at all. But this man was the real deal.

Her grandmother touched her on the arm. "You and Mack seem mighty keen on each other, suga'."

Summer couldn't deny it. "We have gotten close. He's a good man."

"Well, amen to that," Martha said, throwing up her hands. "I'm glad you finally figured that out."

"Memaw, now don't go getting your hopes up about Mack and me. He's a good friend. But we both know that I only have a week or so left on my vacation. I have to get back to New York."

"You might as well just stay another month or two. I mean, April's wedding is coming up and we'll all be there."

Summer noticed her grandmother nodded her head toward Mack when she said that. It would be just like her lovable grandparents to insist he come to the wedding with them. Just so they could throw him and Summer together again.

"I'll miss him," Summer said, not realizing she'd said it out loud until her grandmother turned to stare up at her.

"You're in love, aren't you?" Martha asked in a hopeful tone.

Summer tried to find a reasonable answer to that question. "I…I don't know," she admitted. "Does love feel like fifty drums beating against your rib cage every time he walks by? Does it make you want to laugh and cry all at the same time?"

"Oh, yes, ma'am. You've got it bad, I'd say," Martha replied. Then she smiled. "Don't worry, honey. I'm not going to spill your secret. This is for you and Mack to work out."

"Oh, so now that you'd made me admit that, you're just going to back off?"

"I did my part by keeping y'all busy together," Martha replied with a wink. "It's up to you how you handle the rest."

Summer shook her head and laughed. "So this summer will be hailed a success in the matchmaking department, huh? First, Mr. Maroney and Mrs. Hanes—the whole place has been watching that developing courtship. And now Mack and me. No wonder the folks living here are always smiling. You are all a very nosy, but well-meaning bunch."

"We just love happy endings," Martha replied, her expression smug as a bug. Then she turned serious. "You know, honey, a lot of people move in here after losing a loved one. They're lonely and bitter. They think their lives are over. The staff is wonderful about keeping seniors involved. We love all the trips Cissie takes us on, and we love the activities Pamela helps us with. But sometimes, what we really need is companionship. So those of us who are still blessed with spouses try to help the widows and widowers out a bit."

"And the occasional wayward relative, too, apparently," Summer said, love for her grandmother coloring her world in a golden hue of appreciation. "Thanks, Memaw. I know your being here has added a lot to the lives of the other residents. And visiting you here has certainly been the highlight of my vacation."

"I do my part, as I said." Martha whirled around and fairly danced her way out to the gathering crowd in the gardens. "Hurry, honey. This shindig is about to get started."

Summer stood back, wondering how her grandmother had known something she would have never believed herself. She had fallen in love with Mack Riley. When had it happened? They'd argued on just about every aspect of this festival, including everything from what kind of food to serve to what kind of chairs to set out. But in the end, they'd always managed to reach a satisfying compromise on how this day would turn out. Somewhere in all that playful disagreeing and serious getting-to-know each other, Summer had started relying on Mack for more than just planning a big get-together. He made her smile. He made her happy. And she really liked it when he kissed her.

That acknowledgment caused Summer to stop and consider all that falling in love meant to her. This was different from what she'd had with Brad. That had been a kind of obsession, a need to have someone watching movies with her on lonely nights, someone to go out to dinner with, someone to show off to friends. But it had been a facade. And Brad had shattered that delicate illusion when he'd turned nasty on her and made her see that all her words of wisdom and all her years of training could also be shattered in a heartbeat.

That would never happen with Mack. Mack was an honest, hardworking man. He didn't seem to have a dark side. With Mack, she'd seen the kind of man she'd dreamed about. A man much like her late Uncle Stuart and her Uncle Richard. A man very much like her father in that when he loved, he loved with all his heart. All of them, her father, her uncles, and now Mack, had the qualities that brought Summer comfort and security. They all always did the right thing, even when they had their own burdens to bear. Even her rolling-stone father had his good points, Summer reminded herself. She'd learned that in coming home. James had done a lot of behind-the-scenes work to make sure her grandparents were always taken care of. Mack was the same way.

Mack would never let her down, or turn mean on her the way Brad had. Mack was honest. No illusions there.

But what would happen to her newfound feelings for him when she had to return to New York? Would they survive a long-distance relationship? And did she even have the courage to tell him that she loved him?

Summer wished she could just blurt her thoughts out to someone. But everyone was busy outside. She didn't have time to write a long e-mail or make a phone call to her cousins. She thought about her mother, but Elsie had been quiet since their spat the other day. Summer felt guilty now. It would be hard to go to her mother for advice when she'd just condemned the woman regarding Elsie's own problems.

As she was leaving her grandmother's apartment, Summer saw the Bible lying on the coffee table. Then she remembered Mack's words to her about God. Was God there to listen to Summer's fears and dreams? Did Christ forgive those who'd strayed from his fold?

Summer stood by the counter, then closed her eyes as she gripped the cool white tiles. *Lord, I know it's been a while. But so much has happened since I came home. I needed to find peace again. I needed to find my soul again. And I did, here where I was nurtured and loved by my grandparents. And I also found a real love, Lord. I think I've found that perfect love that my grandmother believes in. Help me to accept this, Lord. Help me to heal. And help me to learn to love my parents, no matter what.*

The back door opened, causing Summer to blink and turn on her sneakers.

Surprised to find her father standing there, Summer motioned him in. "Hi, Daddy."

"Hey, yourself." James held his cowboy hat in his hand. "Honey, can we talk?"

"Sure," Summer said, wondering why he looked so glum. "Did you and Mama have a fight?"

"No, not exactly," James replied. "We had a good long talk. I told her about…well, you know."

"About your glory days being over, about the possibility of your permanent retirement?"

"Yeah, that." James looked so uncomfortable, Summer's heart went out to him.

"How did she take it?"

"It was the strangest thing. She almost seemed relieved." He shrugged, stared down at the floor. "She hugged me good and tight and laughed and cried and… well, let's just say that things have improved greatly between us."

"I'm so glad," Summer said, meaning it. But she wondered if this meant they'd be leaving again soon, too.

"I just wanted to thank you," James said. "You kept telling me to talk to her. You know I've never been much of a talker."

"Yes, I do know that." Summer could see now that all those times she'd thought her father didn't care, he simply just didn't know how to express himself. "I understand that now, Daddy."

"Do you, really?"

Seeing the hope in his eyes, Summer nodded. "I've been too harsh on you and Mama. I judged unfairly all these years."

"We did you wrong, honey."

His gentle admission melted Summer's heart. "You're here now. That counts in my book."

James rushed toward her then, grabbing her up in a bear hug. "I think I'm going to stay for a while. A good long while."

"I'm glad," Summer said, the lump in her throat burning through her own guilt and misgivings.

"You could, too, you know."

Surprised, she pulled back. "You mean, stay here in Athens?"

"Why, sure. Makes sense that all the flock should just come back together. I know it would make your grandparents happy. And your mama and me, too."

Summer turned away, unable to look her father in the eye. "I'd have to think long and hard about that. April has moved back and I do miss her. But I can't leave Autumn up in New York all by herself."

"It is a lot to think on," James said. "What about Mack, though?"

Summer pivoted, lifting her eyebrows. "I thought you weren't so keen on him."

"I like Mack," James said, palms up. "And he seems mighty keen on you."

"It's complicated," Summer said. "I'm not sure."

James nodded, put his hat back on. "Well, that's your call, suga'." He turned, his hand on the screened door. "I just wanted you to know things are better with your mother and me. And that I approve of Mack."

"Thanks," Summer said, touched at his tentative attempts to be a real father to her. Waiting until after James had gone back out, she pushed a hand over her hair and let out a sigh. Then she gathered her things to head out to the party, the sounds of laughter and shouts echoing over the yard and buildings. "Looks like the fun has already begun," she mumbled, smiling.

She looked up to find Mack walking toward her.

"Hi," he said, waving to her.

"Hi." She suddenly felt confused and at a loss for words.

"Everything is in place," he said, a look of admiration on his face. "You did a great job."

"I had lots of help," she replied, putting on her sunshades and floppy red hat. "Thanks for everything, Mack."

He blocked the way from the patio to the yard, his eyes holding hers. "You look great."

"Thanks." She wore baggy denim walking shorts and a bright red-white-and-blue patterned sleeveless blouse. "It's a perfect day, in spite of the heat."

"Yes, it is."

He pulled her close then. "And tonight, I want you with me when those fireworks start going off."

"Okay." She lowered her head, afraid he'd see the truth in her eyes, even through her dark glasses.

But Mack touched her face, forcing her

to look at him. "I want you there, because…well, I think the fireworks started
the day I found you broken down on the
side of the road."

Summer felt tears of joy pricking at her
eyes. "I never told you, but my car wasn't
the only thing having a breakdown that
day."

"You didn't have to tell me. I figured
that out pretty much from the get-go."

"And you're still speaking to me?"

"Yes. I like speaking to you. I like being
with you. I like watching the way your
face lights up when your grandfather tells
one of his lame jokes. I like the way you
laugh whenever you're with the residents,
trying to make paper angels and lace doilies. And I really like the way you've taken
them under your wing, offering them
friendship and advice. I like to watch your
face when you're listening to one of them
tell you the same story you've already
heard over and over. You never look bored
or irritated. You always listen as if the person talking is the only person on earth."

Summer shrugged, blushed down to

her toes. "I guess I've made an impression on you."

"You have."

He didn't seem in any hurry to get out to the party. He pulled her away from the door, then tugged her close. "And I especially like kissing you."

"Oh, Mack—"

Her words ended on a sigh as his mouth touched hers. It was a gentle kiss, reassuring and nurturing, promising and enticing. Summer wanted to stay right here in his arms for a very long time. And yet as he kissed her, all of her fears exploded with the calamity of sparklers going off. How could she tell him she loved him, and then just up and leave him?

She lifted her head, her heart fluttering from his touch, all her hopes pinned on his kisses.

"What?" Mack asked, as if he knew she had doubts.

"It's…nothing. I'm just not sure where all of this is going—"

A knock at a door down the way caused Mack to back up. "That's my apartment."

He squinted in the sun. "I can't make out who—"

At his hesitation, Summer looked around to find a tall, attractive brunette standing there with a small, brown-haired boy by her side. Probably one of the resident's family members coming to the party.

"Hello," Summer said, hearing Mack's intake of breath behind her as she walked toward them. "Can I help you?"

"I hope so," the woman said, her tone haughty but cautious. "I'm looking for Mack Riley."

Summer turned to where Mack stood behind a column out of the woman's sight. He looked as if he'd turned into granite. "Mack?"

"I'm here," he said, pushing past Summer to face the woman. "What do you want, Belinda?"

Summer had certainly heard that name before. Then she realized what was going on. This was the woman Mack had left behind in Austin.

Belinda Lewis, the woman who had

broken Mack's heart, was standing at the door with a little boy who looked exactly like Mack Riley.

"Mack, can we talk, please?"

Mack stared at the woman who had left him twisted and broken, a kind of dull shock numbing his system. Then he looked down at the little boy with her and his heart dropped to his feet. He felt sick inside. Because he knew why she had come here.

He saw Summer moving beside him. "I'm going to go out and find my grandmother."

He heard the disappointment, the acceptance, in her words. He wanted to run after her, tell her this was all a surprise to him, tell her he didn't love Belinda. But the boy was standing there looking up at him with such big eyes, Mack could only nod.

"Can we go inside?" Belinda asked.

"No," he said. "I mean, yes, this is my apartment." He motioned to the small patio. "Let me get the door unlocked."

Belinda pulled the child along. "C'mon, Michael."

Mack watched as the child followed her without a word. The boy seemed shy and scared. Mack felt the same way.

He quickly unlocked the door to his apartment, every fiber of his being pulled taut with an intense dread. Could this be his child?

Once inside his apartment, he headed to the kitchen counter then turned. Belinda was waiting just inside the door. "C'mon in," Mack said, aware that he sounded hollow and winded. He took a deep breath, watching Belinda and the child as they took a couple of steps. "Sit down."

Belinda pulled the boy to a nearby chair. "I know this is unexpected, Mack, but I tried to tell you—"

"What do you want?" Mack asked, his eyes on the little boy. The child smiled shyly at him, and something inside Mack's shocked system responded to that smile. "Hey there."

Belinda cleared her throat. "I have some things to tell you, Mack. So don't interrupt until I get it all out, okay?" She motioned to the boy, Michael. "Sweetie, see that television over there? I think it'd be okay if you watch some cartoons while I talk to Mack." Then she looked back to Mack. "Is that all right?"

Mack found the remote and flipped the television until he found the public broadcasting channel, which carried children's programs every morning. "How's that?"

"I wuv this show," Michael said of the singing animals on the screen. He plopped down on bent knees in front of the moving picture.

"Good," Mack replied. Then he turned to Belinda. "What's going on?"

She looked frightened. Her hands were shaking. And for the first time, Mack saw the dark circles underneath her eyes. She'd lost weight, too.

"First," she began, taking another breath, "I wanted to let you know that my father died about six months ago."

"I'm sorry to hear that," Mack said. In spite of how her father had treated him, Mack knew Belinda had loved the man.

"There's more," Belinda said, tears pricking at her eyes. "My mother has remarried and moved to California. I've…been alone for a while now, except for Michael."

Mack took in that information, wondering how Belinda had managed. She and her mother had never seen anything eye to eye, but worse than that, Belinda hated being alone. She sent a glance toward the little boy, making sure he was absorbed in the learning program.

"Michael is three years old, Mack," Belinda said. "And he's your son."

Mack's sharp intake of breath caused Michael to glance around. In a whisper, Mack said, "What do you mean? How can that be?"

Belinda looked embarrassed. "Remember that time after you'd struck out on your own and I came back to you? I wanted us to get back together and get married?"

Mack ran a hand down his face. "I remember. We…we were indiscreet. I thought you were back for good."

"Yes, you thought that. And I used that to my advantage. I threw myself at you."

Mack remembered all of it. He hadn't exactly turned her away. In a moment of weakness, he'd given in to her tempting promises. Just for one night. But that time, he'd been the one to leave. Now he would have to own up to his past mistakes.

"Belinda, are you telling me that you got pregnant that night?"

She nodded, careful not to talk too loudly. "I found out weeks later, but by then I'd found someone else. He seemed to be everything I wanted—he had the clout, the status. We ran in the same social circles. So I married him and made him think the baby was his. We broke up about a year later, after he found out the truth."

Mack swallowed the bile rising in his throat. "Why would you hide my own son from me?"

Belinda shuffled her feet, then crossed her legs, her expensive sandals clicking on the wooden floor. "You know me, Mack. I didn't think you could give me the things I wanted. And I was bitter because of that, so I decided to get even with you by never telling you about Michael. Besides, my daddy forced me to keep the truth from you. He said marriage beneath our family status would be a joke. Better to pretend Michael belonged to my better-suited husband." She laughed, but it sounded sharp-edged and bitter. "Well, now the joke's on me."

Mack watched as she sucked in a sob, his mind reeling with the knowledge that the adorable little boy sitting in front of his television was his. He had a son. "What do you mean?" he finally asked.

"I'm dying," Belinda said, her gaze moving from Mack to the child and back. "I have skin cancer—all those days by the pool finally caught up with me."

Mack closed his eyes, trying to comprehend what she was saying. "Are you sure?"

She nodded, sniffed back tears. "Oh, yes. I'm very sure. I've had three surgeries on spots on my back, but the cancer has spread. I only have a few months."

Mack held to the arms of his chair until his knuckles turned solid white. Then he realized she was wearing a wig that looked so much like her real hair, he hadn't even noticed. "But…you have money and resources and—"

"That doesn't really matter now. Money can't save me. I'm going to California, to be with my mother. She…she loves Michael, but she's not prepared to take him full-time. She'd want visitation rights, but—"

Mack felt his world spinning, felt the whole foundation of his trust and faith being tested. "You mean, you want *me* to take Michael?"

"That's why I'm here," Belinda said. Then she reached for his hand. "I've done so much wrong in my life, Mack. I've hurt a lot of people. Especially you. I was so self-centered. I loved you, but I thought position and money were more important, so I kept stringing you along because there is one thing money can't buy. I didn't want to be alone, so I kept coming back to you until somebody better asked me to marry him. That was a mistake, because he wasn't the better man. Now I don't have time to string anyone along."

She glanced over at Michael. "He'll have a trust fund. I've already met with my lawyers about that. And my mother only asks to visit him and have him visit her. She knows the truth now. She's willing to let you raise Michael, but she really wants to be his grandmother. She'll need him after…after I'm gone."

Mack watched as she held her head in her hands. "I'm so sorry, Mack. For everything. I pushed you that night, and it was wrong. But I don't regret having Michael. I just regret that I never told you the truth."

Mack looked at the woman he'd thought he'd loved. Then he thought about Summer, the woman he'd fallen in love with completely. Belinda had changed. She was trying to make amends before she died. He had to admire her for that, at least.

Then he looked at Michael. His son.

"I have a son," he said. Then he pivoted back to Belinda. "Does he know about me?"

"I've tried to explain things to him, but he's so young. That's why I had to come now. I wanted us to spend some time with you, just in case."

Mack understood what she was saying. He needed to get to know his son before Michael lost his mother. His heart welled up with a father's protective nature. And already, he knew he'd do whatever needed to be done for this little boy. His little boy. He didn't know how to say the words that thanked God and also asked for forgiveness in the same breath. He and Belinda had had a lapse in judgment, but his son wouldn't be punished because of that. Mack loved the boy completely. And he would protect him, no matter what.

Even if it meant he'd have to give up Summer.

He took Belinda's hand. "I can't turn him away. You know that, don't you?"

Belinda smiled. "Yes, I do. I know you will do the right thing, Mack. Because you're that kind of man. At least I knew that all along, in spite of how I treated you."

"And now you're doing what has to be done, for his sake."

She nodded. "About time, don't you think? I just hope I'm not too late."

Mack held her hand in his. "You're not, Belinda. It's never too late to do the right thing."

He just hoped Summer would see it that way too.

Chapter Fifteen

Elsie touched Summer's arm, causing her to jump.

"Mom, you scared me."

"I can see that," Elsie replied, her bright-red lipstick warring with her equally bright-red spangled earrings. "You were so lost in thought. Honey, are you still mad at me?"

Summer turned to her mother, her heart bursting with the need to talk to someone. "It's not you, Mom. I shouldn't have said those things the other day. I know you're trying very hard to make up for the past."

Elsie let out a breath. "Thank goodness. I've been so worried." Then she gave Summer a bittersweet smile. "But something good did come out of our fight."

"Oh, and what's that?" Summer asked, her mind drifting back to where Mack stood talking to Belinda and the little boy.

They'd stayed for the picnic and she'd had to endure watching Mack offer the child everything from a hot dog to cotton candy. She'd had to endure the way Mack looked at Belinda, the way he'd kept her close all day. Now, she watched as he escorted Belinda and the boy to Belinda's car. They were leaving, at last. And she was dying to hear Mack's excuses.

Earlier, he'd rushed by, grabbed her arm, and said, "We need to talk."

Boy, did they ever.

"Honey?"

Summer turned to find Elsie staring at her, her eyes wide with concern.

"Oh, I'm sorry. Just tired. What happened that's so good?"

"Your father and I," Elsie replied, her expression serene and sure. "I told him about our fight and…he finally opened up to me. About why he's been acting so strange."

"He told me that earlier," Summer said, thinking it seemed as if that had been a whole lifetime ago. "I'm so glad he talked to you."

Elsie let out a long sigh. "What I thought was another woman was just your father's insecurities about growing old. Imagine him thinking I'd stop loving him if he isn't out there seeing and being seen. I never did much care about all the travel and all the parties and appearances. I did care about being with your father. And that's all I care about now."

"I take it from the smile on your face, that he told you he's not having an affair, and that you two aren't getting a divorce."

Elsie waved a hand, her navy silk blouse shimmering in the growing dusk. "No, no. I was only imagining all that. Your father has been depressed, Summer. Since Stuart's death, he's seen his own life differently, I guess. He was afraid I'd be the one to leave him, if you can believe that."

Summer gave her mother her complete

attention. "No, I can't begin to believe that. You love him too much." Her words brought a shard of pain etching across her nerve endings. She loved Mack. But she could see him drifting back to Belinda. He'd shown her that today. And she had a feeling there was much, much more to the story.

"I do love your father," Elsie said. "I'm sure he told you this earlier, but…he knows it's time for him to give up the road, honey. He's tired. He wants to settle down and rest some, but he was worried about how to tell me that. He actually thought I'd be disappointed in him. He thought once we stopped traveling around for all his business commitments and all his doings with the rodeo circuit, that I'd get bored and want to leave him. I just can't see how that man got such a notion." Then she let out a laugh. "Of course, I was thinking the same thing about him."

Summer could see it. She'd seen it too many times in her line of work. "People change, Mom. Things change. Getting old can be a very stressful thing. It's hard for some people to accept. I'm so glad you and Daddy have talked things out. You can grow old gracefully, and together."

Elsie wiped at tiny tears. "Yes. Now I'm looking forward to it, darlin'. I'm so glad we had this time with you. I...I was so afraid it was too late—with both your father and with you. Now I have hope, Summer. So much hope."

Summer hugged her mother close. "I'm so glad, Mom. Daddy loves you. You know that. And I love you."

Elsie squeezed Summer, holding her tight. "Oh, honey, you don't know how much it means to hear you say that. I love you, too. And I promise you this. I will always be right here in Athens from now on, if you ever need me."

Summer felt her heart opening to that promise. "What about right now, Mama?"

Elsie stood back, her gaze moving over Summer. "What's wrong?"

Summer motioned toward where Mack was leaning into the car door, saying goodbye to Belinda. "That," she said. "I think

Mack's old flame has rekindled the spark with him."

Elsie squinted toward the sunset. "I wondered who that was. I thought maybe it was his sister, or something."

"Or something," Summer said, whirling to go and sit on her grandmother's patio. She'd had enough of picnics and bandstands. She'd had enough of bean-bag tosses and dunking booths. And she'd had enough of watching Mack with another woman all day.

Elsie followed her and settled down beside her. Then the door to the apartment opened and Martha came out onto the porch. "Well, there you are," she said to Summer. Then she searched the crowd out in the yard. "Who is that woman who's been with Mack all day?"

Elsie patted the chair next to her. "Summer needs to talk to us, Mama."

Martha hurried to the chair. "Tell us, honey. You've looked so lost and sad all day. Did something go wrong with Mack and you?"

Summer looked down at her sneakered

feet. "That's his old girlfriend. She showed up first thing this morning." She took a deep, ragged breath. "And I think that little boy might belong to Mack."

Both her mother and her grandmother gasped.

"That can't be," Martha said, staring hard into the gathering twilight. "Mack's never mentioned a child. I mean, Mack is solid. He wouldn't abandon his own child." She looked from Summer to Elsie. "Would he?"

"That's the burning question," Summer said, suddenly realizing her grandmother had voiced the very thing that had been nagging at her all day. Had Mack abandoned the boy? Was Belinda here because of that abandonment?

"I can't believe this," Elsie said, her tone full of regret and condemnation. "And just when I thought you'd found the perfect match."

Summer got up, leaned against the white wooden railing. "Mack and I were tentative at best, Mom. Things were headed in that direction, but let's face it, we had a lot to work through. My work in New York is a big factor. And I'm not sure a longdistance relationship is what either of us want. And now this—"

Martha made a sound of distress. "You have to talk to him, Summer. I'm sure there is a reason for this."

Elsie nodded. "That might not even be his child."

Summer looked out into the crowd. "It's about time for the fireworks. I'd better go check with the pyrotechs and make sure everything is in order. Y'all should find Papaw and Daddy and enjoy the show together."

Elsie took her hand, pulling her back. "Summer, don't let this ruin things. You and I—we've come so far. Don't turn bitter on me again. Promise me that."

Martha took her other hand. "She's right, honey. You came home in a mood, and even though you've never talked about it, I have to believe your work was just about to do you in. You needed a rest. And you do look rested and happy, or at least you did up until now. We love you,

Summer. We're here to help you through this. And God will help you, too."

"Thanks, Memaw." Summer shook her head. "This is between Mack and me, but you're right. Only God can give me the answers I need on how to handle this. But I am bitter. And angry. I trusted him. I didn't think he had any secrets." Then she remembered he'd never actually told her everything about his time with Belinda. Was this the rest of the story? "How could he not tell me this?" she asked. "How could he keep something so important from me?"

"This is a biggie," Elsie said. "Maybe he was embarrassed or ashamed. Maybe he was waiting till the right time to tell you."

"Maybe," Summer replied, her soul bruised and battered. She remembered Mack saying there was more, that he needed to tell her the whole story. Was this what he'd kept from her? It felt as if she'd been slapped. But this time, it wasn't by a man's hand. It was by Mack's deception instead. That hurt almost as much as the night Brad had hit her.

Summer willed herself to be strong. She'd kicked Brad straight out of her life that night, and got a restraining order put against him. She wouldn't take any man's abuse ever again, whether it be physical or mental. And if all of this were true, if that precious little boy belonged to Mack, then he'd not only abused her trust. He'd broken her heart. And that was one wound that would never heal.

Mack stood apart from the crowd, watching as the sun set to the west over the lake. Out in the water, the ducks and geese squawked their disapproval of all the humans milling around the complex grounds. He closed his eyes and held fast to the sounds of the waterfowl, to the sounds of laughter floating out over the still, warm night. He held fast to the picture of family and friends, of friendships and fellowship.

Today should have been a good day. A perfect day. And so it had been to the many residents and guests who'd come to share in the celebration and the fireworks.

But Mack had been miserable all day. Miserable at times, he corrected. At other times, he'd looked down at the trusting face of the little boy who belonged to him, and a kind of piercing joy had shattered his heart, filling it with light and love even as it filled it with regret and remorse.

He had a son.

He was in love with Summer.

Belinda was dying.

In the flash of a summer sun ray, his whole life had changed completely, taking a one-eighty turn that meant nothing would ever be the same.

He'd put off talking to Summer. But it had to be done. Their whole relationship would have to be put on hold. And Mack was so afraid that their growing feelings wouldn't survive that kind of holding pattern.

"Only one way to find out," he said as he turned to look for her. She'd stayed away, distant and quiet, since this morning. He knew she was imagining all kinds of vile things about him. Some of them he deserved. And some of them he had to explain. If she'd listen.

Then he saw her.

She was walking toward him, her long golden hair flying out in a haphazard ponytail around her head and shoulders. Her shoulders slumped as she tucked her hands into the deep pockets of her baggy walking shorts. Her head was down. She looked defeated. She looked as if she'd already given up on them.

Mack aimed to change all of that. Somehow.

He closed his eyes again, and asked God to give him the guidance he so desperately needed right now. He'd made a big mistake, but Michael wouldn't suffer because of that mistake. Belinda had come to him, all pride gone now, and asked him to take their child. There was no question Mack would do that. He'd love Michael and raise him and he'd abide by Belinda's request. Michael would never suffer because of the past.

Michael would be his future.

Somehow, he had to find a way to have Summer in that future, too.

So he opened his eyes and looked at her.

"Hi," he said, reaching out a hand as she approached.

She took his hand, her whole being hesitant and restrained. "It's time for the fireworks."

He nodded. "And you're here with me, in spite of everything." That gave him hope.

"You said we need to talk."

He squeezed her fingers. "There is so much to say."

She slanted her head, looked up at him. "He's your child, isn't he?"

"Yes."

The silence was shattered with the first bright white and red bursts of color in the night sky.

"So, are you and Belinda—"

"She's dying, Summer. She came here to ask me to take Michael."

He heard her gasp, but it was soon drowned out by the second burst of color in the sky. Greens, pinks and purples this time. Bright and beautiful and arched to the heavens.

Then Summer pulled away, her eyes accusing. "How could you do that, Mack? How could you walk away from your own child?"

Mack's heart dropped like a lead weight, causing him to feel sick at his stomach. She thought…she thought he'd abandoned his own son? Then he understood. Summer had been abandoned so many times by her own parents. Or so she'd believed. Why should she believe anything but that about him. It looked that way, at least.

"Summer, you need to understand—"

"Oh, I understand. I understand that I fell in love with a man who…who left his own child behind to start a new life."

"That's not true."

"Oh, really? Then why haven't you ever mentioned that you had a child, Mack? Did it just slip your mind?"

Anger coursed through Mack's system. Anger and a tiredness that left him searching for breath. In the sky, the fireworks shot out over and over again, breathtaking in their fiery beauty, loud and crashing and stunning in their simplicity.

"I didn't know," he shouted over the boom of the rockets. "Summer, I didn't know I had a son."

She turned toward him, doubt warring with relief on her face. "How could you not know?"

He grabbed her by the hand, dragging her away from the crowds to take her to the one place where he could convince her that he loved her and that he'd never known until today that he had a son.

As the fireworks came to a pounding finale full of starbursts of fire and sparkles of red, white and blue shimmers raining down around them, Mack put her in his truck and headed for the farm.

Summer clung to her side of the truck. She knew Mack well enough to know not to try and talk to him right now. He was taking the asphalt at a high rate of speed, as if he wanted to put some distance between himself and everything that had happened today.

He hadn't known.

That kept crashing over and over in her mind. He hadn't known he'd had a son.

And she had to admit, knowing Mack the way she thought she knew him, that this had to be the truth. He would never leave a child of his behind. Never.

So she waited until he pulled the rickety old pickup into the yard of the farmhouse, her heart bursting like the fireworks they'd just left behind as her childhood home came into focus in the moonlit night.

Mack halted the truck, then came around to open her door. "Get out."

She did, allowing him to take her hand and pull her to the steps of the house. Mack sat down, then he pulled her down beside him. "I'm going to talk, Summer. And I want you to listen. Can you do that for me?"

She nodded, silent and waiting.

He let out a long breath. "Belinda started calling me a couple of weeks ago, just as I mentioned to you. I told her I didn't want to talk to her or see her, but she tracked me down anyway. And now I know why." He stopped, checked to make sure she'd heard him.

Summer nodded. "Go on."

"I knew Michael was my son the minute I saw him. Almost four years ago, Belinda and I had one last encounter. She had me convinced that she'd never leave me again, so I gave in to my need for her." He gave a disgusted grunt. "You know that old saying about hating yourself in the morning? Well, I did.

"This time, I asked *her* to leave. I realized that I couldn't live like that anymore, waiting for her to come back, waiting for her whims to decide what would happen for the rest of my life. So I told her it was over for good this time. I tried to explain why—that I needed a commitment, that I wanted marriage and a family—but she couldn't see things very clearly. She was so angry at me.

"I didn't try to find her after that. I just tried to get on with my life. But she didn't take my rejection too well. She went to her father, complaining that I'd used her and then dumped her. Her father believed her and decided to get even with me for hurting his little girl. He'd never approved of me, and even though Belinda and I were through, I guess he still considered me a threat. Especially since I was becoming more and more successful, which would look good in Belinda's eyes. He thwarted my efforts at every turn. And even though I had a growing business in Austin, one day after I lost a major client because of Mr. Lewis, I just kind of went numb and decided I needed to move on. I think deep down inside, I'd been hoping Belinda would come back to me, but she never did. She married another man and that was that. That's the last I heard of her.

"I left Austin and traveled around the country, working here and there at landscaping firms and doing nursery work when I could. Then I settled here in Athens and tried to put Belinda out of my mind.

"Today, she told me everything. Her marriage didn't work out. The man she married found out about Michael's true parentage. Apparently, at her father's insistence and to protect herself, she had passed Michael off as her husband's, but he couldn't hack it, so he took off."

He took Summer's hand, his eyes locking with hers. "I didn't know, Summer. You have to believe that. I didn't know I had a child. If I had, nothing would have stopped me from taking responsibility for him. And now, Belinda is dying. She only has a few months to live. Her father's dead and her mother's remarried. She wanted me to get to know my son before it's too late. She wants me to raise Michael. I have to do that, Summer. Now that I know the truth, I have to be with my son."

Summer sat there, listening to him, and felt her soul being turned inside out. He was telling her the truth. Because Mack always told the truth. He'd been honest with her from the beginning, so she had no reason to doubt him now. Still, it hurt so much.

"What about us?" she finally asked, her words raw with confusion and pain.

"I don't know," he said, shaking his head. "It's a lot to ask of you. But I want you to understand. I'm going to have to go to California for a while, to be with Michael and Belinda. Her mother is there, and she wants to be with her mother…at the end. She wants Michael to be with people who can help him when things get tough. I have to go, Summer."

Summer nodded, tears forming in her eyes. "I do understand. You can't turn your back on them."

"No, I can't. But I don't want to turn my back on you, either. I love you. I think I've loved you since the day I found you there on the side of the road."

She laughed through her tears. "I was so broken. So confused. And things sure went downhill from there."

He pushed closer to her, taking her against him. "That depends on how you look at things."

"Well, things aren't looking so good from where I'm sitting."

He kissed her tears. "Look at where you're sitting, Summer. You're home. This is the house you came back to. The people you love will always be welcome here. If you're willing to wait, I will be right back here one day, too."

"With your son," she reminded him.

"Yes, with my son. I hope you can accept that."

She shuddered, turned toward his arms. "But…I have to go back to New York. I have to think about all of this."

"I don't want you to leave," he said, his cheek touching hers.

"I have to leave. You need time to…get through this. And so do I."

He nodded, silent as he just held her there. "So are you saying…there's a chance for us, in spite of everything?"

Summer looked up at him, her heart filling with that perfect love she'd tried so hard to understand. "I think there's a good chance. You see, Mack, you are the kind of man a woman can trust. Because you always do the right thing. And taking Michael is the right thing."

He slumped toward her, the relief in his eyes shining through the moonlight. "Loving you is the right thing, too."

"That's debatable, but I like the sound of it. So you go and take care of Michael and I'll…I'll figure out how to resign from my job and come back here to you. Back to you and Golden Vista. Maybe there's a place there for me, if I can get licensed to be a social worker in Texas."

"I think that's a good idea," he said. Then he took her head in his hands. "You're really okay with all of this?"

"I'm getting there. I was so worried. I thought—"

"You thought I'd left Michael behind, like you were left behind so many times."

She bobbed her head. "I was wrong. I'm glad I was wrong." Then she looked up at him. "But there's something I need to say."

"I'm listening."

"It's about me and my own hang-ups. It's about my work. I see abused and battered woman every day, but in my last relationship, I was the one being abused."

Mack's expression changed from loving to protective. "You let a man abuse you?"

"Hard to believe, isn't it?" She sniffed, lifted a hand in the air. "He only hit me once. But that was enough to make me stop and see things very clearly. I had to practice what I preached, so I told him to get out. He left, and he never bothered me again. He knew he'd regret it if he did."

Mack drew her close. "I can back that up."

"You don't need to do that," she said, glad she'd finally told him the truth. "It's over. I've got people watching him very closely. He'd be wise never to hit a woman again." She touched a hand to Mack's face. "But that was part of the reason I took a leave from work and came home. I needed…to find my confidence again. I felt so ashamed, so weak. I'd failed all the women I tried to help."

"You didn't fail," Mack told her. "You did the right thing. You got out of that situation."

"No more wrongs," she whispered. "We were both condemning ourselves for being weak, for being human. But now, we have a chance to make things right."

"No more wrongs," Mack said, cradling her close. "From now on, we work at it until we *do* get it right," he said, moving toward her. "So right. Together."

Summer sank into his embrace, her

mind whirling with all the struggles ahead. This did feel right and perfect and wonderful. And she knew that in spite of everything in their way, it would all turn out the way God had planned for them if they just put their faith and their love first. She hadn't done that with Brad—he would never have agreed to those terms, and she couldn't tolerate his abusive nature. And she certainly hadn't trusted in God's guidance with her parents. But all of that would change now.

Now she knew how to accept the perfect love Christ extended to His flock. Now she knew how to accept the love of a good, strong man who had learned through trial and error how to be a faithful Christian. She deserved that kind of love, even if she didn't feel worthy. But God had shown her she *could* be worthy. She would fight for that honor, for that grace. She would fight for Mack, and her parents and grandparents. And all the residents of Golden Vista.

Summer looked over Mack's shoulder at the house she'd loved and lost. But she still had the heart of this old house. She had her memories and she had all the people she loved here with her.

And now she had Mack and Michael, too. She was home at last, and the view looked perfect.

* * * * *

Dear Reader,

Is there such a thing as a perfect love? Maybe not in this life. But we know we have the perfect love of Christ with us always. That's a lesson Summer Maxwell had to learn in order to find true happiness with Mack Riley.

Mack had failed at love because he tried to be perfect for the wrong woman. Summer had failed at love because she always felt unworthy of receiving love. Together, they had to learn that while human love might not be perfect, it can be complete and fulfilling with a little help from friends, family and especially God.

I hope you enjoy this second book of my TEXAS HEARTS trilogy. Please look for the third and final story in this series, *A Leap of Faith,* when Autumn Maxwell learns that she can depend on faith to help her find her soul mate.

I hope you have God's perfect love in your life to help you through sad times and joyous celebrations.

Until next time, may the angels watch over you—always.

Lenora Worth

If you liked the FAITH ON THE LINE
series from Love Inspired,
you'll love the
FAITH AT THE CROSSROADS *series,*
coming in January from
Love Inspired Suspense!

On sale in January 2006
from Steeple Hill Books.

Brendan Montgomery switched his beeper to vibrate and slid it back inside his shirt pocket. Nothing was going to spoil Manuel DeSantis Vance's first birthday party—and this large Vance and Montgomery gathering—if he could help it.

Peter Vance's puffed-out chest needed little explanation. He was as formidable as any father proudly displaying his beloved child. Peter's wife Emily waited on Manuel's other side, posing for the numerous photographs Yvette Duncan insisted posterity demanded. Apparently posterity was greedy.

Judging by the angle of her camera, Brendan had a hunch Yvette's lens sidetracked from the parents to the cake she'd made for Manuel. Who could blame her?

That intricate train affair must have taken hours to create and assemble and little Manuel obviously appreciated her efforts.

"Make sure you don't chop off their heads this time, Yvette." As the former mayor of Colorado Springs, Frank Montgomery had opinions on everything. And as Yvette's mentor, he'd never been shy about offering her his opinion, especially on all aspects of picture-taking. But since Yvette's camera happened to be the latest in digital technology and Frank had never owned one, Brendan figured most of his uncle's free advice was superfluous and probably useless. But he wouldn't be the one to tell him so.

"Don't tell me what to do, Frank," Yvette ordered, adjusting the camera. "Just put your arm around your wife. Liza, can you get him to smile?" Satisfied, Yvette motioned for Dr. Robert Fletcher and his wife Pamela, who were Manuel's godparents, and their two young sons, to line up behind the birthday boy.

Brendan eased his way into the living room and found a horde of Montgomery and Vance family members lounging around the room, listening to a news report on the big-screen television.

"Alistair Barclay, the British hotel mogul now infamous for his ties to a Latin American drug cartel, died today under suspicious circumstances. Currently in jail, Barclay was accused of running a branch of the notorious crime syndicate right here in Colorado Springs. The drug cartel originated in Venezuela under the direction of kingpin Baltasar Escalante, whose private plane crashed some months ago while he was attempting to escape the CIA. Residents of Colorado Springs have worked long and hard to free their city from the grip of crime—"

"Hey, guys, this is a party. Let's lighten up." Brendan reached out and pressed the mute button, followed by a chorus of groans. "You can listen to the same newscast tonight, but we don't want to spoil Manuel's big day with talk of drug cartels and death, do we?"

His brother Quinn winked and took up his cause. "Yeah, what's happening with that cake, anyway? Are we ever going to eat it? I'm starving."

"So is somebody else, apparently," Yvette said, appearing in the doorway, her flushed face wreathed in a grin. "Manuel already got his thumb onto the train track and now he's covered in black icing. His momma told him he had to wait 'til the mayor gets here, though, so I guess you'll just have to do the same, Quinn."

Good-natured groans filled the room.

"Maxwell Vance has been late since he got elected into office," Fiona Montgomery said, her eyes dancing with fun. "Maybe one of us should give him a call and remind him his grandson is waiting for his birthday cake. In fact, I'll do it myself."

"Leave the mayor alone, Mother. He already knows your opinion on pretty much everything," Brendan said, sharing a grin with Quinn.

"It may be that the mayor has been delayed by some important meeting," Alessandro Donato spoke up from his seat in the corner. "After Thanksgiving, that is the time when city councilors and mayors iron out their budgets, yes?"

"But just yesterday I talked to our mayor about that, in regard to a story I'm doing on city finances." Brendan's cousin Colleen sat cross-legged on the floor, her hair tied back into the eternal ponytail she favored. "He said they hadn't started yet."

Something about the way Alessandro moved when he heard Colleen's comment sent a nerve in Brendan's neck to twitching, enough to make him take a second look at the man. Moving up through the ranks of the FBI after his time as a police officer had only happened because Brendan usually paid attention to that nerve. Right now it was telling him to keep an eye on the tall, lean man named Alessandro, even if he was Lidia Vance's nephew.

There was something about Alessandro that didn't quite fit. What was the story on this guy anyway?

A cell phone chirped. Brendan chuckled when everyone in the room checked their pockets. His grin faded when Alessandro spoke into his phone. His face paled, his body tensed. He murmured one word then listened.

"Hey, something's happening! Turn up the TV, Brendan," Colleen said. Everyone was staring at the screen where a reporter stood in front of City Hall.

Brendan raised the volume.

"Mayor Vance was apparently on his way to a family event when the shot was fired. Excuse me, I'm getting an update." The reporter lifted one hand to press the earpiece closer. "I'm told there may have been more than one shot fired. As I said, at this moment, Maxwell Vance is on his way to the hospital. Witnesses say he was bleeding profusely from his head and chest, though we have no confirmed details. We'll update you as the situation develops."